Gazing into Crystal Balls . . .

Gigi removed another couple of layers. The silken fabric she wore consisted of strips of various sizes that combined to form a solid layer. The more she removed, however, the less that fabric covered. All that remained was two wide pieces. One of them hung loosely from her neck and down the front of her chest while the other was tied about her waist. Beneath the silk, pert, rounded breasts swayed as she moved, and the thatch of hair between her legs became increasingly moist. Clint realized that second fact for himself when she took his hand and guided it between her thighs.

"What?" she whispered. "What don't you like?"

"Right now, I can't think of a damn thing."

She smiled and began unbuckling Clint's belt. "Now that's what I wanted to hear."

THE GUNSMITH

398

DEADLY FORTUNE

J. R. ROBERTS

JOVE BOOKS, NEW YORK

THE BERKLEY PUBLISHING GROUP
Published by the Penguin Group
Penguin Group (USA) LLC
375 Hudson Street, New York, New York 10014

USA • Canada • UK • Ireland • Australia • New Zealand • India • South Africa • China

penguin.com

A Penguin Random House Company

DEADLY FORTUNE

A Jove Book / published by arrangement with the author

For information, address: The Berkley Publishing Group,
a division of Penguin Group (USA) LLC,
375 Hudson Street, New York, New York 10014.

ISBN: 978-0-515-15550-1

PUBLISHING HISTORY
Jove mass-market edition / February 2015

PRINTED IN THE UNITED STATES OF AMERICA

10 9 8 7 6 5 4 3 2 1

Cover illustration by Sergio Giovine.

ONE

Clint Adams didn't think much of the town called Las Primas. The only reason he stopped there at all was to give his Darley Arabian stallion a much-needed drink after a hard day's ride. Since there was a perfectly good trough in front of what looked to be a perfectly good saloon, he shrugged his shoulders and decided to kill two birds with the same stone by slaking his own thirst as well.

"Here you go, boy," he said while tying the stallion's reins to a post and giving his nose a few pats. "Don't get too comfortable, though. I reckon we can still cover plenty of ground before the day is through."

Clint and Eclipse had ridden enough miles together to cross one end of the country to the other and back again. Even though they didn't speak the same language, horse and rider knew each other better than most people Clint had ever met. Huffing and shaking his head, Eclipse put his nose into the cool water and started to drink. Unable to resist the temptation himself, Clint dipped a hand in and then splashed some of the water onto the back of his neck before looking up at the sign hanging near the window. The words SWEET CAROLINE'S SPIRITS were written over the painting of a woman's leg in a black stocking.

"Then again," Clint said to the thirsty stallion, "I might just stay a short while."

Knowing Clint as well as he did, Eclipse wasn't surprised in the least.

As soon as he opened the front door, Clint was greeted by the sounds of a banjo being strummed to a lively melody by a man who gave him a friendly nod. He sat on a stool next to a piano that didn't have a player at the moment and a narrow stage that was about the same length as the bar, which was built against the opposite wall. In between the two structures were tables of varying size and shape. Even though the saloon seemed to have been cobbled together from parts of several other places, none of the customers there seemed to mind one bit. Of course, the women making the rounds among those customers most likely had a hand in keeping smiles etched deeply into all those faces.

The moment Clint stepped inside, he was spotted by one of those women. She had a smoothly rounded figure and long red hair that flowed over one shoulder. Her dress was worn off the shoulders, exposing a generous amount of creamy white skin.

"Well now," she said as she walked up to take his arm, "why haven't I seen you around here?"

"Because I just arrived," Clint replied.

"Consider me the welcoming committee. How about a drink?"

"You read my mind. Now let's see if you can guess what I'm thirsty for."

After tapping her chin in a show of deep concentration, she said, "You look like a man who prefers beer over whiskey."

"I'm impressed."

After bringing Clint over to the bar, the redhead leaned back on it to rest her elbows against the chipped wooden surface. "Now let's see if you can guess what I want."

Clint could almost feel her hungry gaze brushing against him as she slowly ran her eyes down below his belt. "How about I start with the beer and we'll see about the rest in a short while?"

"Don't you forget about me," she said while brushing her hand along Clint's cheek. As soon as she turned away from him, she'd already caught another man's eye and was heading over to try her luck with him.

"No chance of that," Clint said as he watched her hips sway beneath her skirts.

The man behind the bar was a tall fellow with the build of someone who hadn't lifted anything heavier than a full bottle of whiskey in some time. Even though his hair was plastered to his scalp, several clumps still managed to protrude at odd angles. "Did I hear you mention wanting a beer?" he asked.

"You did," Clint replied.

"I got something imported all the way from England. Real dark, thick stuff. Care to give it a try?"

One of the many things Clint liked about California was that even places like this one could acquire any number of fine delicacies brought into any number of ports. "Sure," he said. "Why not?"

The barkeep set a mug onto the bar and then reached down for a clay jug. The stuff he poured from the jug looked as if it had been brewed from tar. There was a bit of light brown foam at the top, which didn't help the beer's appearance in the least. "On second thought . . ." Clint said warily.

Stopping him with a patient nod, the barkeep said, "I know. I thought the same thing myself when I got a look at it. Try a sip, and if you don't care for it, I'll find you something better."

Clint hesitantly picked up the mug. Not only did the beer look as thick as molasses, but it was even heavier than he'd expected. He brought it to his mouth, but stopped short of letting any pass his lips. Instead, he took a few sniffs and was surprised by a rather pleasant scent. Wincing slightly, Clint took a drink.

"Well?" the barkeep asked.

"It's not bad." Clint took one more sip. "Don't know if I'd make a habit of drinking this sort of thing, but I suppose I'll finish off this one."

"I had you pegged as a man with refined tastes!"

"Seems like everyone knew about me before I even got here," Clint mused.

"My name's Barry. If you need anything else, just give me a holler."

Since the barkeep had extended his hand, Clint shook it and introduced himself as well.

"Clint Adams?" Barry said, surprised. "The Gunsmith?"

"That's right."

"Well, it's an honor to meet you, Mr. Adams."

"Call me Clint."

"All right . . . Clint. How long you plan on being in town?"

"Not long at all."

"If you need a room, I've got a few real nice ones for rent upstairs. I can also arrange for someone to keep you company as well."

"Yeah," Clint chuckled. "I gathered that much already."

After putting away his jug of heavy beer, Barry went to check on his other customers.

Clint turned around so he could lean against the bar while gazing out at the rest of the saloon. There were a few card games in progress, which looked to be very small stakes. The banjo player had stopped for the moment so he could fix a broken string. The redhead was having a heated exchange with the man she'd set her sights on. As Clint watched to see if she might need someone to step in on her behalf, he caught sight of two young men who weren't attempting to hide the fact that they were staring at him.

Raising his mug, Clint let those two know that he'd seen them as well. Neither of the younger men responded in kind, but one of them turned to the other to whisper something while hooking a thumb in Clint's direction. Taking another sip of his beer, Clint considered finishing his drink and putting the place behind him just to prevent his pleasant day from taking a turn for the worse.

The two men came to some sort of consensus before they both shifted their focus to Clint's portion of the bar. As they approached him, they put mean scowls on their faces and their hands upon the pistols strapped to their hips.

"So much for a restful drink," Clint sighed.

TWO

The first of the two men to get to Clint was less than an inch taller than him and a few pounds heavier. His wide nose had obviously been broken a few times and yet his rounded cheeks still wouldn't allow him to look like the threat he so obviously wanted to be. Planting his feet and squaring his shoulders to Clint, he asked, "What'd you say your name was?"

"I didn't say," Clint replied. "Not to you anyway."

Judging by the confusion on the young man's face, someone might have thought Clint's response was given in an exotic foreign language. "What's that supposed to mean?" he grunted.

"It means I didn't say anything to you." Nodding toward the second young man, he added, "Or to him. Why don't the two of you find some other way to pass your time?"

The other young man was considerably smaller than the one with the broken nose. He had the wiry features of a small animal that had been trapped in a cellar long enough to eat its weaker relatives. Bony fingers clawed at a rusty Peacemaker in his holster as twitchy eyes fixed upon Clint. "I heard what he told the barkeep. He said his name was Clint Adams."

"That true?" the first man asked.

Before Clint could respond, the second fellow said, "'Course it's true, Paul. I heard him and so did you!"

"I wanna hear it from him," Paul said. "What about it, mister? Are you the Gunsmith?"

Clint took a longer pull from his dark beer, savoring the way it coated his throat. The stuff had a mighty good kick to it as well, which went a long way toward making up for the consistency. "One piece of advice for your friend. What's his name?"

"That's Mose," Paul said. The man with the rodent's features beside him nodded as if he were testifying to some kind of exalted truth.

"All right, Mose. Here's some advice. Try not to introduce yourself with your hand on your gun. That tends to make folks nervous."

Mose shoved Paul aside so he could step up to Clint and leer at him while saying, "Damn right you're nervous. You'd be a fool not to be when you see—"

Clint's hand moved in a flicker of motion that could barely be seen as he reached out and snatched the pistol from Mose's holster. He flipped the gun around and pointed it at its owner, all without taking his eyes from Mose's face.

Paul hopped back to bump against the bar, leaving Mose to stand there slack-jawed as Clint thumbed back the Colt's hammer.

"There," Clint said in a steady voice. "Now we're both nervous. Seems kind of foolish, doesn't it?"

Mose's mouth struggled to form words, but no sound came out. For a second or two, he looked like a beached fish gulping for its next breath. As amusing as the sight was, Clint knew it would only make matters worse if he allowed himself to laugh at the young man.

Spinning the Colt around once again, Clint left the gun dangling from his trigger finger. "Go on," he said. "Take it."

Hesitantly, Mose reached for the pistol. When it wasn't pulled away, he grabbed it and stepped back. He kept his fingers wrapped around the middle of the Colt, reluctant to shift into anything that might be construed as a threat.

"You heard correct. I am Clint Adams. Something I can do for you two?"

Neither of the other two had anything to say.

"If that's the case, I suppose I'll be on my way," Clint said. "I'd say it was good to meet you, but that'd be a bald-faced lie." With that, Clint tipped his hat to them and turned to walk out the door.

Every step of the way, Clint expected to hear movement behind him. He couldn't get a hint as to what Paul and Mose were doing from the other customers since they'd been too wrapped up in their own affairs to notice there'd been any friction between the three men at the bar in the first place.

Once he was outside, Clint stopped and immediately stepped to one side of the door. Then, he put his back against the wall and crossed his arms while taking a look up and down the street. The only thing there that caught his eye was Eclipse, who was still drinking as if he had every intention of draining the trough dry.

Clint didn't have to wait long before the saloon's door was pulled open again. Paul was the first one to step outside.

At first, he seemed puzzled since Clint wasn't in front of him but he quickly spotted him standing nearby.

"Shit," he grunted in surprise while making a quick grab for his pistol.

Leaning into him, Clint snapped his right fist out to catch Paul on the chin. When Paul staggered forward while grabbing his face, Clint kicked his knee as if he were cracking a low fence rail in two. Paul's leg didn't break so easily, but it came out from under him quick enough. Mose was next to come through the saloon's door, and since Paul had dropped no more than a step past the threshold, it was all he could do to keep from tripping over him on his way out.

Mose already had his gun drawn, which made it easy for Clint to decide which arm to grab. Clamping both hands around Mose's wrist, he pulled the slender man away from the door, continuing in a semicircle to fling Mose into the wall. Mose's chest impacted hard enough to shake the nearby window in its frame. Disarming him after that was a simple matter of Clint removing the Colt from Mose's loose grip.

"Since you can't seem to hang on to this Peacemaker," Clint said, "I'll keep it for you."

Mose stood with his face a few inches away from the wall to which he'd just been introduced, too stunned to do much else. That left a scant few options for Paul. Naturally, he chose the wrong one by drawing his pistol as soon as he'd pulled himself up to one knee. Fortunately for Clint, Paul was even slower after getting knocked down and tripped over than he'd been at any other time.

Clint's boot came down onto Paul's wrist, pinning it to the boardwalk that ran outside the saloon's main entrance.

He then reached down and tapped the barrel of the Peacemaker against Paul's temple just hard enough to draw his attention.

"You make one more move as stupid as that one and I'll give you another knock," Clint warned him. "Believe me when I tell you the next one won't be nearly as gentle as the first."

Having regained what little sense he had, Mose turned around and said, "Give me back my gun!"

"Or what?" Clint asked. "You'll hurt me some more? Oh, wait. I'm the only one here who hasn't been hurt just yet. There goes that threat. Care to try your luck with another?"

As Mose fumbled with the effort of coming up with a retort, Paul said, "This was a mistake."

Removing his boot from Paul's wrist, Clint offered him his free hand while saying, "Now that's the first smart thing you've said in what I imagine has been a hell of a long time."

"We can still do this," Mose snarled. "It ain't too late."

"Shut your damn mouth," Paul said.

"What are you two talking about?" Clint asked.

Ignoring Clint completely, Mose fixed his eyes intently on Paul and said, "She told us we could do this! It's all we got."

"What seems to be the problem here?" asked a man who'd decided to wander up to the small group in front of the saloon.

Clint looked over at the man who'd just spoken, fully prepared to tell him to get the hell out of his sight. He thought better about that when he noticed the tin star pinned to that man's shirt.

"No problem here, Sheriff," Clint said.

The lawman's lanky build and thick, wide mustache made him look like a broom that had come to life and been given the job of keeping the peace in a small town. Narrowing his dark blue eyes, he said, "Doesn't seem that way to me. That man's bleeding."

Since both Paul and Mose were slightly worse for wear, Clint wasn't certain which of them the sheriff was referencing. "Just a friendly disagreement," he said. "Isn't that right?"

"Yeah," Paul sighed. "That's all it is."

The sheriff looked at each of the three men in turn. "You sure about that?"

"I was just about to suggest settling the matter with a drink," Clint said.

"Good," the sheriff said. "You're making a disturbance out here. Move along."

Clint tapped the brim of his hat in a casual salute. "No problem."

THREE

Even though Mose was still unsteady on his feet, he was less than thrilled to be sitting down. He continued griping under his breath as Paul and Clint took seats of their own around the same table inside the saloon.

"Back already?" the bartender hollered from his post.

Clint nodded. "I'll have another one of those beers. Actually, bring some for my friends here as well."

"Coming right up!"

"I don't want a beer," Mose snapped.

"Take it and shut the hell up," Paul snarled.

"But I ain't thirsty."

"Then do us all a favor and drown yourself in it."

"My guess is that the two of you aren't exactly the best of friends," Clint mused. "From the amount of venom in your tone, I'd say you're brothers."

Paul glared at Clint. "Look, you got the drop on us without taking a scratch for yourself. What do you want by keeping us here?"

"I'd like to know what the hell you two were thinking when you stepped up to me in the first place."

"Thought you were someone else, is all."

"No," Clint said. "You called me by name."

"You mentioned it to the bartender and we overheard."

"Right, so you know damn well who I am."

"What's that matter? I imagine plenty of folks know who you are."

"That's right and the ones who introduce themselves the way you two did aren't normally out to strike up a new correspondence with someone."

"You think you're so smart with all them fancy words," Mose said through gritted teeth.

The banjo player launched into a spirited rendition of "O! Susanna" as Paul said, "Shut up, Mose."

"You got lucky, Adams," Mose continued. "That's all and I bet that's the only reason anyone knows who you are."

"I told you to shut up. Do it. Now."

As the two men bickered, Clint merely sat back and quietly waited for the beers to be brought over to the table by a young lady with her black hair tied into two braids. After sipping the dark brew, Clint nodded his approval over to the man who'd poured the drinks.

"Told you, didn't I?" Barry said.

"Yes, you did," Clint replied. When he put the mug down, Clint noticed that the other two men at the table with him were now the ones keeping quiet. "You two through snapping at each other?" Clint asked. "I'd say if I was wrong about you being brothers, the only option left is that you're married."

"You plan on keeping us here?" Paul asked.

"I'm no lawman," Clint told him. "I couldn't arrest you if I wanted to . . . which I don't."

Paul's eyes wandered to the modified Colt holstered at Clint's side. Tucked beneath that same gun belt was the Peacemaker that had been confiscated during the recent scuffle.

"Oh, I almost forgot," Clint said as he pulled the Peacemaker from his belt and slapped it down on the middle of the table. "Go on and take it."

Neither of the men at that table with Clint was inclined to accept that offer.

Taking advantage of the nervousness he'd fostered in them, Clint asked, "Who's the woman that told you to come after me?"

"What woman?" Paul asked.

"When we were talking before, you mentioned something along the lines that 'she' said you could do this and that it was your only chance."

"I don't recall saying that."

"That's because he did," Clint said while pointing across the table at Mose. "And don't treat me like an idiot. Who's 'she'?"

Mose shifted as though a campfire had been lit under his chair. Even though he didn't look like he was about to say anything, the expression on his face said more than enough.

Paul noticed that as well and sighed at his partner's terrible poker face. "You won't know her," he said.

"I know plenty of people," Clint said. "Try me."

"Her name is . . ." Paul glanced over to Mose, rolled his eyes, and let out another labored sigh. "Her name is Madame Giselle."

"She run a whorehouse around here?" Clint asked.

"No."

"Sounds like the name of a woman who'd run a whorehouse."

"Maybe so, but she don't run a damn whorehouse," Paul snarled. "She works down the street."

"Opium den?" Clint asked.

"No!"

"I can probably come up with a few more guesses based on her name, but it'll be easier if you just told me."

"This has gone on far enough," Mose said. "We don't have to sit here and tell this man a damn thing."

The only part of Clint that moved was his eyes as they shifted in their sockets to look at Mose. When he spoke, his lips barely even wavered. "You will sit there and you will answer my questions. It's the least you could do to make up for the fact that you came at me with your gun drawn for no good reason."

Placing both hands on the table, Mose pushed his chair back and got to his feet. "Then I suppose I'm runnin' low on courtesy because I'm fixin' to leave anyway."

"If respect or manners don't mean a thing to you, then what about self-preservation?"

"You threatening me?" Mose growled unconvincingly.

"Call it what you like," Clint replied. "All I'm saying is that, considering how we were first introduced to each other, it makes perfect sense for me to assume you'll try to take another run at me. That means I should gun you down before that happens. That could be the next time we cross paths, or it could very well be if you try to storm away from this here table."

Mose may have tried to keep a mean look on his face,

but it was crumbling faster than a thin coat of old paint in a hailstorm.

"Sit your ass down," Paul said. "Ain't no reason for this to get any worse." When Mose didn't obey right away, Paul put him in his place with nothing more than an angry stare. Averting his eyes as if he was embarrassed by his partner as well as what he was about to say, Paul told Clint, "Madame Giselle is a fortune-teller."

"You mean . . . like a palm reader?" Clint asked.

Paul nodded. "Among other things."

"Why would she send you after me?"

"She didn't send us after you specifically. We asked if we could find a way to prove ourselves to Mr. Torquelan, and she said we would if'n we spent enough time at this here saloon."

"She said a man would come who had a big name," Mose said. "Clint Adams is a mighty big name."

"Depends on who you ask," Clint said.

"If you ask us," Paul said, "it is."

"I'd be flattered under different circumstances. Who's this Torquelan fellow?"

Paul squinted at Clint. "You sayin' you don't know him?"

Before Clint could respond, Mose said, "I thought you were here for him. You sayin' you're not?"

"I'm saying I don't even know who he is," Clint said. "Now could one of you, I don't care which, tell me?"

"Mr. Torquelan is a prospector," Paul said.

Clint waited to hear more. When nothing else was offered, he asked, "That's it?"

"He gathers claims and puts them under one roof, so to speak."

"And how does he acquire these claims?"

"However he can manage, I suppose," Paul replied. "I don't exactly have a head for figures and such."

"No, you're gunhands." They were inept gunhands, but Clint kept that part to himself for the sake of speeding this conversation along. "And if you were looking to impress this Torquelan fellow by coming after me, I have to figure he hires gunhands to work for him."

Paul nodded.

"I get the picture." Clint had plenty of other questions, but doubted the two idiots in front of him could answer them. More than that, he was sick of looking at them so he said, "You two get out of my sight."

Mose began to reach for the pistol on the table, but stopped short so he could look to Clint.

"I'll leave it with the barkeep," Clint told him. "Come back for it while I'm not here."

Nodding, Mose followed his partner out of the saloon.

Clint sighed and scooped up the Peacemaker so he could head over to the bar. "Keep this safe until its owner comes back, would you?"

"Sure thing," Barry replied cheerily.

"One question," Clint said as he leaned against the bar. "What do you know about a man named Torquelan?"

"Enough to know it's not good for business to talk about him behind his back."

FOUR

When Clint had broached the subject of Madame Giselle, Barry had been much more willing to talk. In fact, his face lit up a bit as he gave him directions to the fortune-teller's place of business. Even though it wasn't very far from the saloon, Clint decided to ride Eclipse over there rather than leave the stallion where he'd been tethered. As it turned out, that was the best choice he could have made.

No two streets of Las Primas were the same size. Some were wide enough for two carriages to pass each other comfortably, and others were barely wide enough for a man to get past a horse without being knocked aside. The section of town where Clint was headed was crowded to the point of being nearly impassable. Storefronts were pressed together like the baffles of an accordion. Vendor carts and tents clogged the street and blocked alleyways, making the district feel like it was about to spill out into the surrounding parts of town.

If Clint had been on foot, he wouldn't have been able

to see much through the constant barrage of people, fluttering tent flaps, and smoke coming from any number of
cooking fires started by salesmen who lived in their tents
or stalls. Even with the height he gained by being in the
saddle, it still wasn't easy to see past all the commotion
closing in on him from all sides. Barry's directions had
told him to go down this street about halfway and look for
a man selling fish. At that moment, Clint could barely tell
whether he was halfway down the street or still at one end
of it. Since there wasn't enough room to turn Eclipse
around, he pressed forward.

Every step he took was a fight for territory. People con-
stantly bumped against him and the Darley Arabian in an
attempt to draw his attention. Some of them were just being
jostled by others, who knocked them around like balls inside
a child's toy. When the scent of fish caught his nose, Clint
followed the pungent odor to the left side of the street.
Because he could see above the heads of the women clustered
nearby trying to sell cheap necklaces, Clint was able to spot
the little wooden stall displaying several fish dangling from
hooks.

"Pardon me," Clint said to a confused man who'd just
realized his pocket had been picked.

"Excuse me," Clint said to some of the women selling
necklaces.

Before he could get past those women, a few of their
competitors selling even cheaper jewelry came along to
close the gap. "Make way," Clint told them. Only half of
the women listened to him and the other half cursed at
him when he rode past them anyway.

"This is no place for a damn horse!" someone shouted.

Clint couldn't see who was hollering at him, so he

turned in the general direction from which the voice had come and said, "Then I'll be on my way if I can just find somewhere to go!"

When he twisted around in his saddle, Clint had only been trying to make sure he hadn't accidentally trampled someone or knocked anyone over. As chaotic as the street felt to him, most everyone on it with him seemed to be much more accustomed to the insanity. Despite the complaints and raised voices, the people moved when they had to and came together again to continue whatever they'd been doing. Once Clint had moved along, they found other targets for their shouted complaints.

Apart from noticing those things, Clint also spotted one man in the crowd who wasn't complaining or being affected in the slightest by his surroundings. He stood like a post driven into the ground with a river flowing around him. In the quick look he'd gotten, Clint was almost certain that man was staring directly at him.

"Watch where you're going!" a hoarse voice scolded.

Clint shifted back around to see that Eclipse had taken it upon himself to veer to one side and had almost pushed over the fish vendor's cart. "Sorry about that," Clint said.

The fish vendor grunted something in Spanish and reached out to swat Eclipse's rump to get him moving a little faster.

"Hands to yourself!" Clint roared.

Some of the fish vendor's next words may have been an apology as he chopped off the head of a salmon, but he grumbled them too softly to be heard.

When Clint turned back around to try and find the man who'd been watching him, the river of people had swallowed him up. After taking a few more steps, Eclipse was able to slow to a stop without being prodded or poked. Clint took a breath and was rewarded by the sight of a small tent with fringe around the upper edges and a small square banner hanging above the entrance flap. On the banner was painted a picture of an open hand with a crystal ball resting on its palm. Even though there were no words on the sign, Clint was certain he'd found the place he was after.

After climbing down from his saddle, Clint tied Eclipse's reins to the closest post he could find and then walked toward the tent. It was about half the size of a modest cabin and had a fragrant smoke drifting out through a small crease between the flap and the banner. Clint reached for the flap, pulled it aside, and spotted a bulky figure standing less than two paces beyond the entrance.

"Hello?" Clint said tentatively.

The figure turned around to point a shotgun at Clint's chest.

FIVE

Clint held his hands where they could be seen while keeping them close enough to reach for his holster at a moment's notice. "Easy now," he said. "If this is a bad time, I can come back."

"Who the hell are you?" the man with the shotgun asked. He stood only an inch or two taller than Clint, but seemed like a giant while inside the confines of the tent. He had a doughy face and thin, stringy hair that was so light in color it seemed closer to white than blond.

"I'm just a customer. The name's—"

"It's all right, Patrick," a woman said as she stepped around the big man. She was about a foot shorter than the man with the shotgun and had a smooth, rounded face framed by thick waves of dark hair. She reached up to touch his arm, displaying delicate fingers with nails painted dark red. Looking to Clint, she said, "That is, unless I've misjudged you."

"As long as your judgment tells you not to point a shotgun at me," Clint said, "it's correct."

Reluctantly, Patrick lowered the shotgun. Studying Clint carefully, he said, "He ain't one of them that was here before."

"I can see that," the woman said. "Who might you be, mister?"

"I'm Clint Adams." When he spoke, he watched for anything in the woman's face or mannerisms that might tell him she was any sort of trouble for him. From what he could tell, she didn't even recognize his name.

Holding out one hand, she said, "Pleased to meet you, Clint. I'm Madame Giselle. What brings you here?"

"Thought I'd duck into this tent before I got trampled by that crowd outside," he told her.

She laughed and showed him a smile that made the effort of fighting through the locals to be completely worth the trouble. "I know how you feel. It's quite overwhelming, especially for someone new in town. When did you arrive?"

"Just today. In fact, I hadn't intended on staying longer than it took to have a drink and maybe a meal." Taking in the sight of the shapely curves beneath the filmy silk clothing she wore, he added, "Glad I didn't leave town, though."

When she shook Clint's hand, Madame Giselle did it as if she were wrapping herself around him. Even though her fingers were the only part of her wrapping around anything, Clint could feel it all the way down to his toes. "I am, too," she said. "What brings you here today? Do you have specific questions or are you simply curious?"

"Oh, I definitely have specific questions."

Raising her eyebrows, she said, "I like a decisive man. Why don't you come inside?"

Clint was more than happy to watch Madame Giselle turn and reach for the curtain behind her, but wasn't quite so eager to follow her through it. When she turned back around to check on him, he asked, "Do you greet all of your customers by having a shotgun pointed at them?"

"I was hoping you'd overlook that."

"Easier said than done."

Despite the difference in their heights, Patrick genuinely recoiled when Madame Giselle shifted her gaze toward him. She softened considerably by the time she was looking once again at Clint. "There was a bit of trouble with some recent customers," she said.

"Didn't like what their futures held?" Clint asked.

"In my line of work, trying to shoot the messenger is more than a turn of phrase."

"I've had the job of unwelcome messenger a few times myself. Never pleasant."

"Indeed. Would you like to come in? If my partner's misstep where the shotgun was concerned has spoiled you on the idea, I completely understand."

Clint looked over to Patrick. Although the big fellow didn't shrink from him the way he had from Madame Giselle, there didn't seem to be cause for alarm. Not yet anyway. "I suppose we're all entitled to making mistakes. Would asking for an apology be out of line?"

"Yes," Patrick replied.

Smirking, Clint said, "I'd rather hear that than a half-hearted platitude. After you, ma'am."

Madame Giselle accepted Clint's courtesy with a bow of her head and walked through the doorway into the next portion of the tent. When Clint followed her, he was surprised by the fact that the room was at least three times bigger than he thought it should have been.

"Now this is a damn good trick!" he said as he looked around the spacious quarters containing bookshelves, cabinets, side tables with all manner of relics and charms, a few small altars, and a larger table in the middle of the room that could comfortably host a poker game for five men but had only two chairs at the moment.

"Are you talking about getting my hands on incense that is normally only found in Tibet?" she replied. Directing some of the smoke rising from a small stick resting in a specially shaped bowl, she added, "One of the vendors down the street truly doesn't know what he's got or he would double his prices."

"No," Clint said. "I'm talking about fitting all this furniture into a tent that's half the size of this room."

"Oh, that's easy. I just brought it in through the house." After taking a moment to relish the perplexed look on Clint's face, she peeled back a dark purple curtain to reveal a wooden floor and ceiling that had been sawn apart. "This building was falling down and I bought it for a song. Instead of putting the place back together again, I had one wall partially rebuilt and set my tent in front of the hole. That way I get to conduct my business without the wind blowing the Tarot cards off my table."

"And," Clint added, "you can put your back to a wall instead of a sheet of canvas."

"There's that, too," she said while settling into one of the padded chairs at the table. Motioning to the chair across from her, she said, "Please, have a seat."

Clint sat.

"You mentioned you had specific questions," she said.

"I did."

"What are they?"

"First of all," Clint said as he crossed one leg over the other and rested his hand within easy reach of his holster, "why did you send two men to kill me?"

SIX

After a few seconds of silence, Madame Giselle said, "I beg your pardon?"

"You heard me."

"Did you say you think I sent someone to kill you?"

Clint nodded.

She leaned back in her chair. When she glanced toward the flap leading to the portion of the tent where Patrick was waiting, Clint's hand inched a bit closer to his pistol. He doubted she noticed and he felt badly for preparing to draw with an unarmed woman about, but he'd weathered too many storms to let his guard down when he spotted dark clouds on the horizon.

"Why on earth would I want to harm you, Mr. Adams? We've only just met."

"That's pretty close to the question I asked, ma'am."

She smiled in a surprisingly warm and genuine way. "Since you've come all this way to accuse me of trying to kill you, there's no need to be so formal. Please, call me Gigi."

"All right, then, Gigi. Would you mind answering me or do I need to pay?"

"Anyone who walks in through my door has to pay for answers, but I'll give you this one for free. I don't know who you are, Mr. Adams, and I have no reason to want to see any harm come to that pretty face of yours."

"Since we're not standing on formalities, you might as well call me Clint."

Gigi folded her hands on the table and stared at Clint like the head of a large company sizing up an employee at the bottom of the ladder. "What makes you think I'd have any part in trying to kill anyone?"

"A pair of men came at me in a saloon not too far from here. They were out for blood. My blood, to be exact."

"By the looks of you, it doesn't seem they were much of a threat."

"They weren't. Fact is, I'm surprised they were able to come at me without tripping over their own feet in the process."

"Then what's the problem?" she asked. "No harm done. For all you know, they were drunk and looking to stir up some trouble just to pass the time. Stranger things have happened in saloons, from what I've heard."

"The problem," Clint said with as much patience as he could muster, "is that those men told me they were sent by you and the only thing that kept me from catching a bullet or a knife in the back was their own stupidity."

For a moment, it seemed Gigi was going to claim her innocence one more time. Then, she let out a short breath and placed her hands flat upon the table. She pushed her chair back, stood up, and went to a nearby shelf to select one of several crystal spheres. Her hands caressed each one in turn, and when she looked over her shoulder at Clint, she smiled as if her hands were feeling a part of him instead.

"Plenty of men come to me," she said.

"I can imagine."

"I know what you're thinking, and yes," Gigi told him as she walked back to the table with the sphere in her hands, "they do come to me for that as well." The room was lit by a few lanterns placed on the tables. One of those was directly behind her now and its light had no trouble making it through the thin layers of silk she wore. Her rounded hips and swaying breasts moved freely beneath the material, unencumbered by any sort of restrictive undergarments.

Without making the first attempt to hide the way his eyes drank in the sight of her, Clint said, "It doesn't take a mind reader to guess what I'm thinking right about now."

She sat down and carefully placed the sphere in the middle of the table upon a stand that Clint hadn't even noticed before. Placing her hands on either side of the sphere, she asked, "What do you see?"

"This isn't what I came for," Clint told her. "Just talk to me without a bunch of riddles or mystical nonsense."

"I'm trying to answer your question, Clint. Just tell me what you see."

He sighed and looked at the sphere. This wasn't the first time he'd seen a fortune-teller or someone claiming to have the ability to reach the great beyond. While he'd experienced some things he couldn't quite explain, he had yet to find any reason to believe in the power of crystal balls.

"I see a reflection of your hands," he said. "There's also bright spots in the glass from the lanterns."

Gigi nodded. "And what if I told you the light you see isn't from the lanterns, but from a spirit who's trying to contact us right now?"

"I'd have to say it's mighty strange that a spirit that was able to pull off a trick like that looks so much like lantern light."

"You're not a believer."

"How'd you guess?"

"Most of the men who come in here and sit in that chair," she said while motioning to Clint's side of the table, "aren't so doubtful. When they look into one of my crystals, watch me decipher patterns in tea leaves, or gather smoke from my incense, they might be able to see a great many things."

"No doubt they're helped along by suggestions from you."

The tone in Gigi's voice lost the lyrical quality she'd had a moment ago when she said, "Of course. That's part of my job. The men you're talking about . . . was one of them a bit taller than you with darker skin and an ugly nose?"

"Yep."

"And the other," Gigi said while placing a finger to her temple and closing her eyes in contemplation, "was very thin. He wasn't so bright. His name was . . . Mose."

"I knew you could be reasonable if you tried."

Placing her hands once more on the table in front of her, she said, "You've got to admit, that did sound at least a little mystical when I added the rhyme."

"Maybe a little. What did you tell those two idiots when they came to see you?"

"Most men who come here are looking for help with one of two things," she replied while opening a drawer built on her side of the table. Gigi took a deck of cards from the drawer, closed it, and shuffled them expertly. "They're either wanting money or love. Sure, every now and then someone comes along looking for something a bit more heartfelt, but it usually boils down to those first two things."

"Love isn't heartfelt?" Clint asked.

"Not what most men call love. Anyway, the two you're asking about wanted money. More specifically, they wanted to know what they could do to gain some influence within their particular social circle."

"And they told you they were gunhands?"

Gigi shrugged while flipping the cards down in front of her. They were Tarot cards painted with pictures of men on horseback, maidens holding wooden staffs, and arrangements of golden cups. "No, but they obviously weren't farmers. I told them what they wanted to hear."

"Which was?"

"Which was that they would get an opportunity to prove themselves very soon if they just kept their eyes open for it."

"According to them," Clint said, "you also told them they wouldn't get another chance if this one slipped past them."

She flipped over another card and placed it across one of the others. "You met them. They're idiots. How many chances do you think they'd get? For that matter, how many chances do you think they'd be smart enough to spot? I told them they needed to take full advantage of the chance they were given." Fluttering her eyelashes, Gigi asked, "Isn't that true for all of us?"

Clint got to his feet. "The chance they spotted was trying to shoot me to impress a man who wants to hire gunmen. And since they thought they needed to seize their opportunity with both hands, they came after me twice."

Placing her finger once more to her temple, she closed her eyes. "My guardian from the cosmos tells me they did not succeed."

"Right. I'm standing here unharmed so they obviously didn't shoot me. How about telling me whatever else you can in regard to those two men."

"Why? It doesn't seem like they're a threat to you."

"Because I want to know if there will be more where they came from."

"Of course there will be more," she told him. "Even you know that."

She'd spoken that little prediction without a hint of showmanship. Because of that and the fact that it hit so close to the mark, Clint was taken aback for a moment. He recovered quickly enough and walked around the table. Before he got close enough to lay a finger on Gigi, he heard Patrick come stomping into the room.

"The man they were looking to impress is named Torquelan," Clint said. "What do you know about him?"

"Time for you to go," Patrick said.

"Not until you answer me!"

Gigi stood up and held a hand out toward Patrick to keep the big man from making a move against Clint. "Come back later," she told him.

"Why?"

"Because tempers are flaring and that doesn't lead to good things."

Clint didn't need to be a fortune-teller to know that much either. Even though he wasn't particularly threatened by Patrick or the shotgun he wielded so clumsily, Clint wasn't eager to lock horns with him if it could be avoided. "Fine," he said. "I'll come back in a few hours."

"That will give me some time to put my ear to the ground and see what I can learn about the men you seek."

"Whatever you say," Clint replied. He'd had enough of her theatrical talk, and the smell of that incense was making him queasy.

SEVEN

Although Clint agreed that the three of them could use a bit of time to cool off and regroup, he didn't want to run the risk of letting Madame Giselle get too far out of his sight. Fortunately, there were enough vendors of different sorts within a stone's throw of her tent that he didn't have to go far to get the few things he needed.

First, he wanted a place for Eclipse that was safer than the spot where he'd tied the Darley Arabian behind the fish vendor's stall. There were several small lots that were being used as corrals and he was able to convince the owner of one of them to part with some space and some feed. They weren't the best accommodations, but they would suffice. Since the lot was wedged in among so many other carts and tents, nobody could make off with Eclipse without creating a commotion anyway.

Next, Clint had to tend to a more basic need. His stomach had begun to rumble so much that the scents that had induced cringes before had become downright appetizing.

Clint wasn't hungry enough to risk eating any of the fish hanging from the stall of the vendor he'd passed on his way to Giselle's, but there was another cart across the street from her that caught his eye.

"Something smells good over here," he said as he approached the cart.

The woman who worked there had long black hair that was shot through with gray. Her features were a mix of Chinese and Indian and the decorations adorning her simple brown blouse were carved from small bits of wood. She smiled at him and picked up some of her wares to show him. In each hand, she held narrow sticks with hunks of cooked meat skewered on them.

"What's that?" Clint asked.

She smiled wider and held the skewers out toward him even more.

"Got anything that's not on a stick?" Clint asked.

She either didn't speak English or didn't know the value of bartering with customers because the woman merely nodded and picked another pair of skewers to show him.

Before taking anything from her, Clint leaned forward to take a sniff of what was on one of the skewers. "What is that?"

Although the woman squinted harder at Clint's face, that didn't seem to help her understand him any better when he asked the question a second time. Finally, the course of action she chose was to set down one of the skewers and try again with another from her modest selection.

"Eh, to hell with it," Clint grumbled. "I'm hungry and that smells good." He took both skewers from her hands, paid her the amount of money she asked for by pointing to a little sign nailed to her cart, and walked away. The street was busy, but

Clint was becoming used to the constant flow of people and horses. His ears had even begun to filter out a portion of the commotion so he didn't feel as if his head would explode from everything being crammed into it at once.

Once he'd found a spot where he could stand without being jostled too much, Clint took a bite from one of the skewers he'd purchased. The meat on that stick was stringy and slightly overcooked. However, it had been marinated in a tangy sauce made from a blend of spices that Clint couldn't quite place. That mystery, along with the hunger that had compelled him to make the purchase in the first place, kept him going until he'd almost cleaned off the second skewer.

"I heard something you might wanna know."

Clint had seen the man approaching him from the left and assumed he would just keep walking. When he didn't, he didn't think much of it. Someone who'd been the target of as many bullets as Clint Adams tended to develop a sense of when another was about to fly his way. More important than any sixth sense, on the other hand, was the fact that this man wasn't wearing a gun and simply had a pleasant face.

"Are you another fortune-teller?" Clint asked.

Looking toward Madame Giselle's tent, the man chuckled and replied, "No! I meant about what you're eating there. I heard a thing or two about it."

Clint pulled off one of two remaining hunks of meat and popped it into his mouth. "What've you heard?"

"It ain't beef."

"I could've told you as much."

"Could be rabbit," the man said.

"No. It's not rabbit."

"I heard it could also be dog."

Clint ate the last bit and tossed the skewer away.

"Whatever the hell it was, it was damn tasty. Now what can you tell me about that piece of meat over there?"

Following Clint's line of sight, the man asked, "You mean the one with the blue scarf?"

"That's the one."

"Never seen him before."

"Are you new in town?" Clint asked.

"I been here since before most of these here stores were built. How new is that?"

"Any idea why he'd be staring this way?"

"Maybe he caught a glimpse of Madame Giselle walking by one of her windows," the man offered. "Sometimes when the light catches the glass just right, you can see her splashing water on her neck. May sound like a simple thing, but I'm tellin' you it's inspirational."

"I have no doubt about that," Clint replied. "Is there law around here?"

"Sheriff doesn't bother coming here unless he's asked."

"Why am I not surprised?" Clint looked over at the man and said, "Would you mind going over and finding out what the hell he wants and why he's staring at me?"

Apparently, the man had run fresh out of things to say because he shrugged and walked off.

Now that he'd finished his meal, Clint was ready to do something other than stand downwind of the fish vendor and watch Gigi's tent flap in the breeze. The first thing he did was look around for another vendor that had caught his eye some time ago. Clint found the vendor, made his way over to him, and then tripped over something or other that had been left on the ground by any one of a number of careless souls nearby.

EIGHT

The man wearing the blue scarf hadn't been standing in the same spot all afternoon. He'd picked three spots and rotated through them at irregular intervals. When he'd made his last shift, he glanced back to the last place he'd seen Clint and quickly realized he could no longer find him. The man straightened up and looked around in a hurry. Once he came up empty in that regard, his eyes settled back on the cart where he'd seen Clint trip and momentarily leave his sight.

Two seconds later, Clint separated himself from the milling crowd to approach him. He stopped about two paces away from the man and smiled. "Doesn't make sense, does it?" Clint asked.

"What?"

"When you lose something and can't find it, you always go back and search at least one more time in the place it should be. And the harder you look," Clint added as he tapped his finger against the brim of the hat he'd bought from the vendor he'd so theatrically tripped in front of not too long ago, "the less you see."

There was no need for Clint to point out the simple hat switch he'd performed. The angry look on the face of the man with the scarf told him that the switch had been noticed all too well if only a little late.

"You're Mason, right?" Clint asked.

Now that did come as a surprise to the man in the scarf. His eyes narrowed into suspicious slits as he gave Clint a single nod.

"The fellow who sold me the hat told me your name," Clint continued. "He didn't have much else to say about you, apart from the possibility that you might work for a man by the name of Torquelan. But then again, I think we both know that's more than a possibility, don't we?"

"You wanna stay alive and healthy?" Mason asked. "You'd best leave town and do it quick."

"Is that so?"

Once again, Mason nodded.

"And I suppose that order comes from Mr. Torquelan, whoever the hell he is?"

"Mr. Torquelan don't give orders. He makes requests and it's a wise policy to give him what he wants."

"All right. So what's he requesting of me?"

"I don't believe he's met you yet," Mason said.

Clint had yet to draw his modified Colt from its holster, but placing his hand upon its grip was more than enough to send the message he wanted. "You're following me for a reason. What is it?"

"I heard your name mentioned. Thought I'd come around to see if it was really you."

"Do I even need to ask who mentioned me?" Clint asked.

Mason grinned. "I believe you already made his acquaintance—at Madame Giselle's."

"That's what I thought. So now we've met. What have I done to deserve being told to get out of town?"

"Just offering friendly advice, is all," Mason replied. "You mind answering a question for me?"

"We're just having a friendly conversation. No harm in that."

"You don't strike me as the superstitious sort. Why would you pay a visit to that fortune-teller?"

"I'm a man of many parts." Raising his eyebrow, Clint added, "Madame Giselle has some interesting parts as well."

"Yes. Indeed she does. She's no whore, though."

"I know."

"So that still leaves me wondering why you were there."

"Why's it so important to you?" Clint asked.

"It ain't."

Even before those words had left Mason's mouth, Clint knew they weren't true. He also had a real good suspicion that it wouldn't do him much good if he confronted Mason with that fact. So for the time being, he let the other man continue as if he wasn't playing with at least some of his cards showing.

Another question came to Clint's mind. Instead of asking it straightaway, he fished for an answer of a different sort. Tightening his grip on the Colt's handle, Clint tensed the muscles in his arm and narrowed his eyes a bit.

"You don't wanna do that," Mason warned.

"I don't like being followed," Clint told him.

"I didn't lift a finger against you, Adams. There's no harm in keeping my distance and watching to see who walks down my streets."

Clint looked at his immediate surroundings to find that folks were still going about their business. Even the people who were close enough to hear what was being said between the two men weren't interested enough to slow their pace to hear any more. What interested Clint the most was that he couldn't see anyone else who was standing still, watching him, or responding to the aggressive stance he'd taken.

Relaxing his grip on the Colt, Clint allowed the pistol to settle back into his holster before saying, "I'd like a chance to meet this Torquelan fellow."

"Why?"

"Because his name keeps cropping up, which means he must be important around here."

"Are you planning on staying in Las Primas for long?" Mason asked.

"At least a few days. Besides, I've already been recognized, attacked, and watched from a distance since I've gotten here. It's been my experience to not treat that sort of thing very lightly."

Sighing as if he were arguing with a stubborn bill collector instead of an armed man, Mason said, "For Christ's sake, I can't believe your nose is bent so far out of shape just because you caught me staring at you for too damn long."

"It's not about that," Clint assured him. "Not entirely anyway. I've made it through many a year by recognizing good opportunities when I see them. Mr. Torquelan sounds like a man who might be good to know."

When Mason stared at Clint, it was plain to see that he was sizing him up in much the same way that Clint had sized him up earlier. "What'd you have in mind?"

"Nothing specific. If someone looking to impress Torquelan takes it upon themselves to come at me the way those two idiots did in the saloon, then perhaps it might be good for me to have a word with him myself."

"I doubt he had anything to do with them two trying to do you harm. At least, in any direct capacity."

"Just let him know I'm interested in introducing myself to him and let me know what he says." Stepping away from Mason, Clint stopped and added, "I'm sure you'll be able to find me again."

Mason didn't have much to say to that apart from a few grunts. He turned away from Clint and headed down the street in the direction that would take him back toward the saloon district. Clint put his back to the closest wall and watched Mason disappear into the constant flow of noisy people.

If there was anyone else in the area who was acting as Mason's partner, he was doing a damn good job of keeping his head down because Clint didn't spot anyone who fit that description. Nobody took much notice of him, and those who did simply studied him like any other prospective customer or mark for a small theft. Clint wasn't worried about either of those so he moseyed down the street in the opposite direction Mason had chosen. There was an old woman selling cakes nearby and Clint was still a little hungry.

NINE

Clint took a long, winding path that allowed him to get a good feel for the busy merchant district as well as the area around it. There wasn't much to the town, but he felt more comfortable having a general feel for the place. After that walk, he made his way back to the fishing vendor's cart from a different angle. The man working there didn't have any trouble spotting him.

"You gonna buy something this time?" he asked in a thick European accent.

"You sell anything other than fish?" Clint asked.

"No."

"Then I probably won't be buying anything."

"Then get away from my cart! You're frightening people with money to spend."

Clint looked around. Although there were always plenty of people to be found in that part of town, none of them were coming within spitting distance of the cart. "Yeah, I'd best clear out so the stampede can start."

"You know who enjoys the company of a smart-ass? Nobody! That's who."

Since Clint couldn't argue with that point, he walked past the fish vendor and went directly to Madame Giselle's tent. Before he got there, he stood back and examined the place from a distance. The house wasn't being hidden behind the tent, but was positioned in such a way that made it tough for him to see that it and the tent were connected.

When he stepped into the tent, Clint was greeted by a familiar face as well as an equally familiar shotgun. "Hello, Patrick," Clint said. "Is the lady of the house in?"

"She is, but you'll wait here," Patrick replied.

"We already made our introductions and seem to be on friendly terms. I can see myself in."

Although he lowered the shotgun, Patrick stepped in front of Clint to stop him like a brick wall. "Folks don't generally walk in that way."

"Is that why you keep pointing that shotgun at me?"

"Well . . . yes. People tend to stand outside and call for someone to come out for them."

Clint nodded. "This is your place and I didn't intend on strutting around like I own it. Let me know what the proper procedure is and I'll abide by it."

Now that he'd been given some measure of respect, Patrick didn't seem nearly as prickly. "It'd do just fine if you announced yourself before walking in. That way I won't be so jumpy."

"Should I walk out and come back in the right way?" Clint asked.

Patrick chuckled a bit and used the barrel of the shotgun to scratch the side of his leg. "No need for that. Madame

Giselle is in there with a customer right now," he said while nodding back to the flap leading to the next room.

Now that he'd let a few seconds pass without speaking, Clint could hear the muted voices coming from the other side of the flap. He couldn't make out exact words, but whoever was in there with her was worked up about something or other. "It really was rude of me to storm in here this way. My apologies."

"Never mind. I'd appreciate an announcement next time, is all."

"Not a problem. Tell me something," Clint said. "Why do you keep the shotgun in hand? I can see why you might have one around in case it's needed, but I have yet to see you without it."

"Some of the men that come here don't want their palms read. They've gotten a look at Miss Giselle and . . . well . . . I'm sure you can imagine."

"Yes, I can. There has to be something other than that, though."

Patrick's face twisted into the expression of a man who'd been pondering something and was just about to part with whatever it was that he'd concluded. Before he could follow all the way through on that, however, the voices from the next room rose to the tone of a normal conversation.

"If you're not happy with what I've given you," Gigi said, "all I can say is I am only a channel through which the spirits flow."

"And I say I didn't get what I came for," the customer replied. Judging by the sound of his voice, Clint pictured him to be a gnarled old-timer with sunbaked leather for skin.

"But I did provide a reading," Gigi continued. "That's what you asked of me. Just because you didn't like what the spirits had to say . . ."

"It ain't that! Dammit, all I wanted was to know where that old bitch hid my money!"

Patrick sneered quietly in a way that caused his upper lip to peel back like a dog baring its teeth.

"I didn't get my money," the customer grunted from the next room. "So you sure as hell ain't getting—"

When the customer fell silent so quickly, Patrick brought his shotgun up.

After another second passed, Clint reached for his Colt.

A split second after that, Patrick had pulled the flap aside and was charging into the next room. Clint was right behind him, amazed at how fast the big fellow could move when the need arose.

In the next room, they found Gigi and a slender man somewhere in his late forties. He had matted red hair, a scarred complexion, and stubble on his chin that looked rough enough to sand a plank of old driftwood down to a silky smoothness. One of his hands had taken hold of the scarves wrapped around Gigi's waist. The other was extending to one side, frozen along with the rest of him due to the little blade being held at his throat.

"Hello, Patrick," she said. Smirking, Gigi added, "And Clint. It's nice to see you, even if it is a little late."

"What's he done to you?" Patrick asked.

Gigi's arm was bent casually as if she were bringing a glass of wine to her customer's lips. Instead, she kept the small dagger, which had a curved, wicked-looking blade, pressed against the redheaded man's neck. "He hasn't done anything to me, not for lack of trying. In fact, Mr. Eastman was about to leave. Isn't that right?"

The redhead, who Clint presumed was Eastman, nodded very carefully. "Y-yeah. I was."

"Good," Gigi said. "Show him out, Patrick."

When Patrick grabbed Eastman by the scruff of his neck and pulled him away, the redhead looked to be more than a little grateful. Once he no longer felt the blade against his neck, however, some of the fire came back into his eyes.

"I'll have my money back," Eastman demanded.

Gigi stepped up to him, holding her knife in an easy grip. The blade was less than three inches long and curved as if specially crafted to fit around a throat or in a man's more intimate crevices. "I think I deserve a bonus for putting up with your foul mouth without cutting it out of your head."

"I'd have to agree with the lady," Clint said as he approached the trio. "What's Madame Giselle's fee?"

"One dollar for a glimpse into the mists of the future," she said.

Clint stuck his hand into Eastman's jacket pockets one at a time. Within the interior pocket, he found a small wad of bills. Peeling off two dollars, Clint held them up for Eastman to see and stuffed the small remaining amount of money back into the other man's jacket.

"I'd say this seems like a fair payment," Clint said.

"Whoever you are," Eastman grunted, "you'd best keep yer nose out of this."

Leaning in a bit closer, Clint fixed Eastman with a stare and said, "This is cheaper than paying a doctor to stitch your empty head back onto your shoulders."

Tougher men than Eastman had buckled under the pressure of that stare. To his credit, he lasted a full second before averting his eyes.

Gigi smiled at Clint as she said, "Patrick, please show Mr. Eastman the door."

"My pleasure," Patrick said. He then shoved Eastman toward the tent flap and didn't stop until the sound of their boots scraping against the ground was swallowed up by the commotion of the street.

"Well now," she said as she walked past Clint to seal the tent flap using a few hooks that fit into rings on the edge of the opening. "It is very good to see you."

TEN

"Can I convince you to stay for a little while?" Gigi asked.

Clint watched her glide away from the door. "I make it a rule not to argue with an armed woman."

She pulled aside one of the scarves around her waist to reveal a little scabbard secreted there. When Gigi brushed the blade against her midsection and slipped it into its leather sheath, she looked as if she could feel the blade like a part of her own body. "What brings you back so early?"

"Thought you might like to know that someone's been keeping their eye on you."

"You mean," she said while stepping up to within an inch of him, "someone other than you?"

"Is that so hard to believe?"

"Not in the slightest," Gigi said, running her hand flat against his chest.

"I met someone out in the street. Name's Mason. Ever hear of him?"

Gigi leaned in close to Clint's ear so she could whisper, "I don't think so."

"I believe he was keeping watch on this place."

"Maybe he was after Patrick."

"Somehow I doubt Patrick is the sort of fellow who attracts much trouble."

"And I am?" she asked.

Clint drew a breath that was filled with the sweet smell of her hair. "Yes," he told her. "You are."

"Then perhaps we should talk somewhere a little more private? For our safety, of course."

"That wouldn't be a bad idea."

Gigi led him into the adjoining house through the door on the opposite side of the room. As he followed her, Clint saw that the entire first floor was sparsely furnished and could almost pass as having been abandoned by its owner. She took him to a set of narrow stairs in what had once been a kitchen and walked to the second floor using steps that made her backside twitch back and forth like a cat's tail.

From what he could see, the second floor wasn't in much better shape than the first. Clint's opinion on that subject changed when he got a look at the room she showed him next.

The air beyond that door was scented with just a hint of perfume and both dressers were carved into delicately curving shapes. Even the floor beneath Clint's feet was something to behold since it was covered in a carpet that must have cost a pretty penny. The centerpiece, however, was a bed that was almost large enough to fill the room. It was covered in a filmy canopy of silk suspended from a hook in the ceiling to drape down around the bed on all sides.

"I'm honored, Clint."

"Why?"

"Because you took it upon yourself to look after my interests. What a gentleman."

"I had my reasons," he said.

"Did you?" Gigi asked as she peeled off the first couple of silken layers wrapped around her body. "And what might those have been?" What she was doing was absolutely mesmermizing.

"I . . . umm . . . don't like . . ."

Gigi removed another couple of layers. The silken fabric she wore consisted of strips of various sizes that combined to form a solid layer. The more she removed, however, the less that fabric covered. All that remained were two wide pieces. One of them hung loosely from her neck to hang down in front of her chest, and the other was tied about her waist. Beneath the silk, pert, rounded breasts swayed as she moved and the thatch of hair between her legs became increasingly moist. Clint realized that second fact for himself when she took his hand and guided it between her thighs.

"What?" she whispered. "What don't you like?"

"Right now, I can't think of a damn thing."

She smiled and began unbuckling Clint's belt. "Now that's what I wanted to hear."

As she worked on removing his clothes, Clint eased his hands along the sides of Gigi's body. Her skin was smoother than the silk she wore, and he couldn't wait to cup her firm breasts. Her nipples grew hard against his palms, and she let out a soft, contented sigh as he massaged her. Soon she had his pants down and was massaging him as well.

Her hands worked expertly on him. She stroked his cock, slowly easing up and down his shaft. Then she brought her hand to her mouth and licked her fingers as if she was enjoying a tasty piece of dessert. When she wrapped her fingers around him again, they were slick and warm. Within seconds, Clint was so hard that he ached. Gigi stepped away from him so she could pull aside the silk curtain and sit on the edge of her bed. Opening her legs wide, she started rubbing her pussy.

"I suppose you saw this in my future?" Clint asked as he removed the rest of his clothes.

Shaking her head, Gigi said, "Not at all. I just couldn't stop thinking about you being inside me."

"Nothing mystical about that."

"That depends. I've got a few tricks I'd like to show you."

ELEVEN

Gigi spread her legs open wide to show Clint her wet pussy. The lips between her thighs were trim and pink, and she ran her fingertips along them slowly while watching him intently. Within seconds, she was trembling with pleasure. The expression on her face had shifted to something more insistent as her fingers worked in a faster rhythm. He could have watched her for a while longer, but didn't have enough patience to keep his distance.

As soon as he was close enough, Gigi reached out for him with her free hand to guide him to her slick little opening. Clint ran his hands along her legs, savoring the way she enveloped him. Her pussy was tight and warm. As he eased into her, he could feel it gripping him as she contracted the muscles between her legs.

Gigi leaned back, keeping her hand between her legs. As Clint moved in and out of her, she continued rubbing herself. Rubbing her lips vigorously, she rubbed Clint's shaft as well, touching every inch of him as he entered her again and again.

"You like that?" she whispered.

"God, yes," Clint replied.

Moving her fingers upward a bit, she found her clit and rubbed even harder. Clint reflexively grabbed her legs in a tighter grip, pumping into her with building force as though he instinctively knew what she wanted. Gigi responded by opening her eyes and watching him as if she couldn't decide if she was going to cry out or just cry. The pleasure she felt was so intense that Clint could feel the muscles quaking beneath her skin.

When she climaxed, Gigi drew a deep breath and held on to it. She closed her eyes and arched her back, putting her pert breasts and rigid nipples on proud display. Clint waited for her to start breathing normally again before sliding out of her and easing her back onto the bed so her legs were no longer dangling over the edge.

He climbed on top of her and immediately felt one of her legs wrap around his waist and one of her hands reach out to start stroking him again. She didn't need to get him erect because he was already there. Instead, Gigi guided his cock to her and rubbed him against her clit. Her skin was even slicker than before, and it wasn't long before Clint was aching to be inside her again. Picking up on his urgency, Gigi kept him from slipping into her for a few more seconds, which were almost more than he could bear. Clint took hold of her wrist and pulled her hand away.

"Why, Mr. Adams, are you forcing yourself on me?" she asked.

"You want me to stop," he replied, "just say the word."

"Stop."

"Why did I know you'd say that?"

Smirking devilishly, Gigi said, "I'm difficult by nature."

"I'm seeing that. Is there any way I can convince you to change your mind?"

"I'd like to see you try."

Clint accepted her challenge without a moment's hesitation. Taking hold of both her hands, he pressed them against the bed and climbed on top of her. She responded by writhing against his body and moaning softly. When he placed his mouth on her nipple and flicked his tongue against her skin, she let out a surprised little sigh.

As he continued to move his tongue against her sensitive flesh, Clint settled in between her legs. He licked between her breasts, all the way up to her neck, while pressing his hard cock against her damp pussy. Gigi rubbed his arms at first, but as soon as she felt his erect shaft against her crotch, she dug her nails into his shoulders and ground her hips in expectation of being penetrated once again.

Clint wasn't about to indulge her. Not just yet. She'd found it amusing to torture him, so now it was her turn.

"Put it in me, Clint," she moaned. "Now."

"You told me to stop," he said while kissing her neck. "That's what I did."

"Now I'm telling you to fuck me."

"I'm not certain you mean it."

She attempted to answer, but was cut short when he bit her just hard enough to catch her attention. Gigi dug her fingernails into him a little deeper and became even wetter between her thighs. "I want you to fuck me," she whispered. "I want it so bad."

Reaching down to guide himself between the moist lips of her pussy, Clint asked, "Is that what you really want?"

"Yes!"

He slipped into her, but had barely put a smile onto her

face before taking it away again. It almost pained him as much as it seemed to pain her when he eased back.

"What are you doing?" she snapped.

"I'm being cautious, since you seem to be having trouble deciding what you want."

"You are a very difficult man. You know that?"

"I've been told," Clint said through a growing smirk. "How about I make it up to you?" With that, he took hold of her hips and flipped her over so she was lying flat on her stomach. Gigi pressed her cheek against the mattress while lifting her backside just enough to get what she wanted. Clint entered her from behind and drove all the way in.

"That's better," she sighed.

Clint ran his hands along her nicely rounded hips as he pumped in and out of her. Positioning himself only slightly better allowed him to bury his cock all the way into her while gripping her hips in both hands. Gigi took a deep breath and held it until he pulled back.

The slope of her back was a sight to behold. Clint moved both hands along her rump, reaching all the way forward until he could cup her breasts. Gigi was the perfect height for him to massage her tits as he started pumping in and out of her again. He quickly fell into a rhythm that made them both forget about the teasing they'd given to each other not so long ago. All Clint cared about was the way her body wrapped around him, and Gigi gripped the sheets tightly while grunting every time their bodies came together.

Soon she tossed her head back to let out a throaty moan. Clint grabbed her tightly, impaling her one last time before his pleasure rose to a boil.

TWELVE

Lying on his back with one foot hanging over the side of Gigi's bed, Clint stared up at a faded tapestry that had been tacked to the ceiling. It took him a while to regain enough strength to put two words together, and when he did, he spoke in a lazy tone.

"Aren't you worried about missing any customers who come along?" he asked.

Gigi lay right beside him on her stomach with one leg bent in a way that made her look like the subject of a painting hung in a saloon. The sheet covered about a quarter of her body, leaving plenty as a feast for Clint's eyes. "They'll come back," she said. "It's not like they can get their future told to them by many others around here."

"I imagine there's a few other tents like this one about."

"Certainly. They don't know what they're talking about, though, and folks around here know it."

"And you do know?" Clint scoffed.

Rolling onto her side to face him, she made no attempt

to cover her bare breasts. In fact, one of her fingers drifted across her pink nipple as she asked, "Are you making fun of me?"

"I wasn't exactly trying to hide it."

"What I do is an art form. People can recognize an artist when they speak to one."

"All right, all right," Clint said, holding up his hands to placate her. "Forget I said anything."

Gigi reached out and grabbed Clint's right hand with impressive speed. She wasn't the slightest bit gentle when she twisted it around so she could look directly at his palm. "Sit still," she told him. "I'll tell you a thing or two."

"Save it," he said while trying to reclaim his hand. "I never pay for a woman's attention."

"I won't charge you. Not for a small glimpse into the mists anyway."

"First sample is free. Common practice for most hucksters."

Since she already had a hold of his hand, Gigi only needed to give it a sharp twist to put a pained expression onto Clint's face. She eased up after a second or two and then rubbed his palm soothingly. "There now," she said. "Let's see what there is to see."

Having already seen plenty of evidence that Gigi could be deadly when that close to a man, Clint decided it would be less painful to just allow her to practice her so-called art.

"Your life line is very deep," she said. "You have seen the face of death many times, but it has not claimed you."

"Since you're not speaking to a corpse, I'd say that's a fairly good guess."

"Your love line is interesting. See all of these branches feeding into the main one?"

"Yes," Clint said without looking at what she was doing.

"Those mean you've taken many lovers. That, combined with a fairly good indication of money, tells me you have a very good life. Full of many trials and lots of blood, but good all the same."

"Is my palm telling you I'm rich?"

"No," she said quickly. "But it does tell me you seldom have to worry about money. That is, apart from the times when you overstay your welcome at a card game. I see that debts to others have brought you into some precarious situations."

Now Clint couldn't help taking a look for himself. "Where the hell are you seeing that?"

She traced her fingertip along various parts of his palm, explaining specific designs and markers that she was seeing there. Being more distracted by her touch than what she was saying, Clint didn't learn much of anything.

"Well," he said, "you're either really some kind of artist or an extraordinary bullshitter."

Putting on a sad pout that was undeniably attractive in her current state of undress, she said, "You still don't believe I can see into the future? Or even the past?"

He answered that with a skeptical scowl.

Gigi shrugged and finally let go of Clint's hand. "I suppose it's a mix of those two things you said before. Even so, I can tell I was hitting pretty close to the mark."

"You were, indeed. Definitely worth the price of a reading."

"Thank you. I can tell that was difficult for you to admit."

"As long as you're giving the reading dressed like you are right now," Clint added, "it's most definitely worth the money."

She looked down as if to remind herself that she was

wearing nothing but the bed sheet that was partially
wrapped around her body. Looking up, she swatted Clint
with the back of her hand. "I can put together a real nice
hex, you know. Something to make you lose your hair or
cause certain parts of you to wither."

"You wouldn't do a thing like that," Clint said as he
climbed on top of her. "Not while you're still using those
parts of mine as well."

"You've got a point there."

He kissed her for a short while, but forced himself to
climb down from the bed before getting too wrapped up
in what they were about to do.

"What's the matter?" she asked. "I haven't hexed you yet."

"What did you find out about that fellow I asked about?"

"Which one?"

"Torquelan," Clint said. "And don't try to tell me you
don't recall me mentioning him. It wasn't that long ago."

Gigi let out a dramatic sigh. "I recall."

After waiting for a few seconds, Clint said, "Well? I'm
listening."

"I don't want to talk about him. Not here anyway."

"Where, then? I've got some things to tell you also."

Perking up, Gigi asked, "Really? What?"

"I'll talk if you do."

She scowled at him and stood up, taking the sheet with
her to use as a makeshift robe. "Let's get something to eat.
I'm hungry."

"I wonder how you worked up that appetite," Clint
chided.

"Don't flatter yourself, Adams."

THIRTEEN

Although they walked only a few streets over from the merchant district, Clint felt as though he was in a whole other world compared to the bustling, vendor-filled chaos of that part of town. Clint's thoughts were brought right back to those cramped quarters when he got a look at the plate that was set in front of him.

Gigi clapped her hands together and smiled down at the food that had been brought to their table. "You won't regret this! Best dinner in Las Primas."

Looking down at their plates, Clint winced. "Fish?" he said. "And not even cooked?"

"It's cooked!" Gigi told him. Glancing to the young man who'd brought the meal, she asked, "Isn't it?"

"Yeah, it's cooked," the server replied. "And if you send it back, the owner won't cook it one second longer so don't even ask."

"I wouldn't dream of it," Gigi said enthusiastically. "I would like some—"

The server produced a shaker of crushed black pepper from the pocket of his apron.

"Ah, yes," Gigi said. "Thank you very much."

"Can I get you anything else?" the server asked.

"How about a nice steak?" Clint replied.

Gigi waggled her hand toward the man standing near the table to shoo the server away. "We're fine," she told him. "When these plates are cleaned off, bring us dessert. The usual."

"What's the usual?" Clint asked.

"Just trust me."

Suddenly growing tired of discussing the menu, Clint waited for the server to go away before saying, "I held my tongue all the way here, just like you asked. You've got your food, so tell me about Torquelan."

Gigi put a forkful of fish into her mouth and chewed it. "I don't know much of anything, I'm afraid."

Shaking his head, Clint told her, "I'm not buying that."

"Didn't think you would. All right, then." She stabbed another bite of fish and brought it most of the way to her mouth before pausing and watching him. "Try the salmon."

Clint was already hungry, so he went ahead and tried it. It wasn't half bad, which meant it must have come from somewhere other than the foul-smelling cart outside Gigi's tent. "It's damn near raw," he griped.

"That's how it's supposed to be. The cook is Japanese."

"That explains it." He dipped the next bite into some of the sauce on the side of his plate, which made a big difference.

"Wilhelm Torquelan is a pig," Gigi said. "He's ruined nearly a dozen families and God only knows how many others that I don't know about."

"Did he ruin your family?"

"No."

"Then how do you know he ruined anyone?" Clint asked.

"Because some of the people he ruined came to me seeking financial advice."

"You'll have to excuse me if I don't put much credence into that."

"This has nothing to do with what I see in the crystals or tea leaves or palms or anything else," she insisted. "I told you people mostly come to me for two reasons."

"Money or love," Clint recited.

"That's right. And I noticed a steady flow of good people coming to me with some very sad stories to tell about losing both of those things."

"What kind of stories?"

Gigi took a deep breath and looked down at her plate as if she didn't remember ordering the food upon it. "The first few came from women who'd lost their sons to violence. I was working in San Francisco at the time and that sort of thing wasn't unheard of. The next few came from men who'd lost their fortunes."

"Nothing new for San Francisco either," Clint pointed out. "Or California in general, for that matter."

"That's what I thought. Also, these stories didn't all come in at the same time or in a row. But then I started noticing patterns. Too many of the stories involved gold men being murdered by killers who moved like a pack of wolves."

Clint found himself picking at the fish more now. The sauce was spicy, but worked well with the flavor of salmon. He didn't dwell on the food, though, focusing instead on what Gigi was telling him. "Again, not altogether unusual for California. What did you mean about a pack of wolves?"

"That's how I saw it."

Leaning forward, Clint asked, "What did you see?"

Closing her eyes, Gigi spoke in a hushed, breathy tone. "I saw not a death stemming from anger or revenge, but from cold calculation. There was more than one killer and they did their jobs well. Like a pack of animals, only not wild. Wolves. With teeth that were—"

"Dammit," Clint groaned. "You're talking about seeing something in your crystals instead of with your own two eyes?"

Her eyelids snapped open and she said, "Not everything I say in that regard is a show. I do have genuine talent, you know. Like any profession, that's what separates the successful practitioners from those who fail."

"We've already established what you practice."

"No. You've established that, but I never agreed. Not completely anyway." Allowing her shoulders to come down from around her ears, she added, "Seeing something using my more exotic methods, when done properly, is just as good as seeing something with my eyes."

"For future reference," Clint said, "when I ask you about something, I'll always be more interested in the latter instead of the former."

"And for future reference," she replied, "I won't ever care about which you prefer."

"Fair enough." Clint could feel his temper starting to flare, so he took another bite of his supper to try and keep it from getting the better of him. Surprisingly, it actually did help. "Is there truly a difference between . . . whatever it is you supposedly see?"

Glancing about at the others seated in the little restaurant, Gigi lowered her voice a bit and said, "Yes. There really is a reason why some people in my line of work can make a good living at it and others don't."

"If only there was a way to tell the difference," Clint mused.

Surely not missing the vague accusation in Clint's words, she told him, "The best way to tell that difference is by looking at the place where a teller gives their readings. If it's somewhere that can be folded up and packed away in under an hour or two, that's probably someone used to leaving town in a rush. Someone with deeper roots has the trust of their neighbors."

"That . . . actually makes sense."

"Why do you look surprised?"

"Because someone who sees tea leaves as anything other than garbage is actually making perfect sense to me." Prodding his supper with his fork, Clint asked, "Did someone poison this fish? Maybe that's why my brain is going soft."

"Do you want to hear the rest of what I have to say or not?" Gigi asked.

Clint took a moment to weigh his options. Since there was still a good portion of his meal to finish, he said, "I'm listening."

FOURTEEN

"That's her," Mason said.

The man standing beside the gunman was about the same size as Mason, but was cut from a completely different cloth. Where Mason had hair that was thinning on top and unruly everywhere else, the second man always looked as if he'd just come from the barber. His features were chiseled and he made his simple, dusty clothes seem fashionable just by wearing them.

Upon hearing Mason, the handsome fellow nodded and asked, "Who's that with her?"

"Clint Adams."

"Are you sure about that?"

"No, Darrow. I pulled that name out of thin air and attached it to the man in there for no good reason."

Darrow looked over at Mason. "There's no need to be rude."

Even though Darrow's voice hadn't risen above what could be considered a polite conversational level, Mason looked rattled by what he'd heard. "That's Clint Adams," he said. "I'm sure of it."

"Why's he with the Pietrov woman?"

"They've been getting friendly of late."

"How friendly?" Darrow asked.

Mason smirked. "I heard a few sounds coming from her house and they sounded real friendly."

"I see. Didn't you say something about one of the others on the payroll getting to this man first?"

"They were two locals," Mason said. "And they're not on the payroll yet."

"They should be," Darrow pointed out.

"Why?"

"Because, if that is Clint Adams, they spotted him before the rest of us did."

Mason grimaced as though he'd just swallowed something rancid. "And if they hadn't acted like a couple of idiots, Adams would have probably left town already. Instead, we've got to worry about him."

"That's a point. Do you think we have anything to worry about?"

Darrow watched for a few more seconds. The expression on his face didn't change. His stance didn't change. His eyes gave nothing away. By all appearances, he could just as well have been watching paint dry. Finally, he said, "We still need to kill her."

"Certain folks will figure we or Mr. Torquelan had something to do with it."

"That's why it should be a messy job. Very messy, in fact."

"That's not how we usually work, but it still won't turn all suspicion away from us."

"It'll turn suspicion in every direction," Darrow said. "At us, at a random cowboy who got drunk and found her in an alley, at some superstitious customer of hers who didn't want to pay for their reading. Everywhere and nowhere. We just need some breathing room. That should give it to us."

Mason sifted through some thoughts of his own before saying, "Mr. Torquelan will probably—"

"Mr. Torquelan put me in charge of this job," Darrow said quickly. "And I'm doing it. We're not going to waste any more time before seeing it through."

"And if it goes bad," Mason added, "you're the one taking the blame."

Darrow shifted just enough to face the man beside him. "What possible good did you think would come from saying that to me?"

"Just making sure we all know where we stand."

"We both already know that. If this goes bad, I would have taken the blame no matter what. Do you suppose that would leave you in the clear?"

Mason didn't have to think for long before chuckling. "I ain't stupid."

"Right. So let's see to it this job gets done, the right people wind up dead, and we all get back to making money."

"Hear, hear."

FIFTEEN

Clint was almost done with his salmon when he asked, "Do you have something to say about Torquelan or not?"

"I do," Gigi replied. "I just wanted to make sure you would listen to me when I told it to you."

"You think I came along this far to ignore you when you finally got around to answering my question?"

Chewing on the last bits of pink salmon mixed in with white rice, she said, "Possibly."

"Would it speed things along if I paid your fee? Maybe then you'd at least speed this along a bit if you treated me like a customer you wanted to get out of your door."

"When you talk like that, I wouldn't mind getting you out of my sight for free," she grumbled.

"You're right," Clint told her. "I'm sorry. That was rude of me."

She batted her eyelashes at him before asking, "Are you just saying that to make me feel better?"

"Partly . . . yes."

Gigi recoiled slightly, but recovered quickly enough. "I suppose there's something to be said for honesty in a man."

"That and I do realize I'm dealing with a mind reader."

Gigi couldn't help laughing. "I never claimed to read minds. Still, since those two did try to hurt you to impress Mr. Torquelan, I suppose you should know who he is."

"Thank you," Clint said.

Pushing her plate aside, Gigi said, "After I met those people who'd run afoul of him and lost someone close to them, things became tougher for me."

"How so?"

"More men tried to kill me."

"More men?"

Gigi nodded. "I'm not as nice to every man as I am to you," she said. "Also, you'd be surprised how many of them don't take it well when you give them news they don't want to hear."

"You could always try to avoid that last part," Clint pointed out.

"You know who also does that sort of thing?"

"No."

"The people who work in those tents I mentioned earlier that are made to be broken down and taken out of town on short notice. And before you make a joke about all fortune-tellers being hucksters," Gigi added, "let me remind you that I'm still carrying that knife hidden on my person."

Clint used his fork to point at her when he said, "I know where you've got that blade hidden."

"You want to bet your life on that?"

"Not particularly."

"Smart man."

"When did these men start trying to kill you?" Clint asked.

"As soon as I told the first one of them that he wasn't going to get back the woman who'd left him or any of the money he'd foolishly spent."

"My mistake. When did the number of those incidents take a sharp increase?"

Gigi smirked. "It was the night after I told someone who'd just struck a deal with Wilhelm Torquelan that he'd see the end of his days before seeing a return on his investment."

"He didn't like that too much, I imagine."

"And Torquelan liked it even less. It was his men who came after me. They told me to amend what I said about him paying what he owed and convince my customer that every spirit in this world and the next would vouch for me."

"And did you?" Clint asked.

"No!"

"You didn't?"

Gigi scowled at him. "Why do you look so surprised?"

"Because you were asked by men who were there to threaten you. Weren't they armed?"

"Yes, they were armed. First of all, someone in my line of work needs to protect her reputation once she builds one that's worth something. And second . . ."

When she didn't finish her sentence, Clint prodded her by saying, "Go on. What was second?"

Gigi let out a short sigh and rolled her eyes as if Clint had already started making fun of her. "I don't like being threatened. When those men came to tell me what to do, the first thing I wanted to do was the opposite. Even if they wanted me to do something I had no objection to."

"I haven't known you for very long and that doesn't surprise me in the least."

"You probably think I'm foolish for doing something like that."

"On the contrary," Clint said. "I've gotten myself into more scrapes than I care to remember because I refused to cater to some blowhard waving his gun around."

"When you're a woman, those blowhards think they can get a whole lot more out of you," Gigi told him in a somber tone. "And considering fortune-tellers get less respect than whores, things get a whole lot worse."

"How bad was it this time?"

"Not too bad." Perhaps knowing that she wasn't lying very well, she added, "I've had worse."

"Did they hurt you?"

"The first time they came around, they were full of nothing but threats. The second time, they shoved me a bit. The third time, things got a bit rougher."

"How rough?"

"That doesn't matter," she replied.

"Come on, Gigi. You've told me this much already. You might as well spill the rest."

"One of them burned me."

Clint studied her carefully. He figured it wasn't too much of a stretch to think she'd play things up to make them seem worse just to get him on her side. A claim like that, on the other hand, seemed a bit extreme for that sort of a lie. "Burned you?" he asked.

"It wasn't that bad."

"Where?"

Reluctantly, Gigi pushed up the sleeve of her blouse to expose her left arm to just past her elbow. There were three circular scars that were about half the size of pennies. One of them could have actually been two scars that had run together. They weren't something he'd noticed before and were only slightly paler than her regular skin tone.

"Are those cigarette burns?" he asked.

She nodded. "They told me they'd do a lot more than that when they came back."

"And did they?"

"I didn't stay around long enough to find out. As soon as they left, I packed up everything I could and left town. Left the entire state, in fact," she told him. "I made it as far north as Oregon, earning as I went. But Lumberjacks and millers aren't nearly as good customers as the folks I found in California, so I came back."

"Smarter money would be on the fact that you came back because you damn well felt like it and weren't about to be told any different."

Although she didn't say anything to that directly, Gigi shrugged and told him plenty with the expression on her face.

"I would've felt the same way," Clint told her. "Nobody should be told where they can or can't make their living. Why would this Torquelan fellow go through so much trouble to get you to change your reading? Do you have that kind of sway with your customers?"

"Not as such," she told him. "But he didn't want anyone at all talking along those lines. He deals in the shadows," Gigi added in the faraway tone that seemed to be reserved for when she was consulting with her spirits. "The money he makes comes from blood and suffering."

"I could've told you as much without even meeting the man," Clint said. "Is there anything you know for certain?"

Snapping back into her regular voice, Gigi said, "Just what everyone else does. He buys up gold claims and deeds to property. I've heard tell that he smuggles illegal cargo into various ports along the coast, but that's about it."

"That's plenty. Are you finished eating?"

"We haven't had dessert, but I don't have any more of an appetite."

SIXTEEN

Clint escorted Gigi out of the restaurant and down the street. The sun had already dipped below the horizon to cast a dull glow over the rooftops on the western side of town. Shadows were stretching out farther along the uneven ground like oil that had been dumped from passing wagons. Although there were plenty of people to be found, Clint spotted a face among them that he wasn't exactly happy to see.

"You still have that blade on you?" he asked.

"Yes. Why?"

"What about any other weapons?"

She stopped and turned to face him. "Clint, what's wrong?"

Placing a hand at the small of her back, Clint moved her along without appearing to be in too much of a hurry. "Remember when I told you someone was watching your tent?"

"Yes," Gigi replied as her muscles tensed.

"Well, there's someone watching us right now. Don't look," Clint said as he gave her another nudge. "Just follow my lead and try to look like nothing's wrong."

When Gigi glanced over at him, she smiled in a way that convinced even Clint that there was nothing bothering her. "Where is he?"

Clint let his gaze wander toward a store's window. Instead of looking at anything displayed behind the glass, he focused on whatever he could see reflected in it. "Close," he said, despite the fact that he couldn't see anything useful in the reflection on the window. "When I give you this signal," he said while tapping the small of her back, "break away from me and find someplace to hide."

"I don't want to leave you to fend for yourself," she said. "I can help you."

"I'm certain you can. When I signal you, though, the best help you'll be able to give me is to get out of my way."

She smiled at him. "I like the sound of that," Gigi purred.

"Good," Clint said as he looked into a wide alley containing a short row of carts that were sealed up tight. "Where's this lead?"

"Across to Vestibule Street," she told him. "There's some nice hotels and a man who builds carriages down that way."

"What about the sheriff? Might he be somewhere in that area?"

Having already turned to stroll down that alley, Gigi took Clint's arm and said, "Sheriff Wheeler is a useless lump of a man. There are a couple saloons near his office a few streets down in the other direction. That's where you'll find him."

"Perfect." With that, Clint gave her the signal.

Gigi broke away from him and headed for a doorway set into the building to her right. She was testing the door to see if it was locked when Clint turned away from her to spin around and put his back to the wall on the opposite side of the alley near one of the carts. Once he'd picked his spot, Clint stayed perfectly still and waited for his target.

The first man to walk past the alley was some chubby fellow with a cane and a monocle wedged in front on his left eye. The next was the tall gunman with the misaligned nose.

"Hello, Paul," Clint said.

Paul's eyes snapped over to him. The surprise on his face made it clear that he could very well have walked down the entire length of that alley without knowing Clint had stopped to wait for him. Now that he had seen him, however, he reached for the gun at his hip.

SEVENTEEN

Having seen Paul fight once before, Clint gambled that he wouldn't be much of a threat with a pistol. That gamble paid off when Clint managed to get away from the wall and several feet to one side before Paul's weapon cleared leather. Even though he no longer had Clint in his sights, Paul still pulled his trigger as soon as he could. The smoke wagon spat its cargo through the air amid a gritty cloud of burnt gunpowder. The noise exploded up and down the alley, rattling Paul even further.

Clint rushed at him from another angle, grabbing Paul's wrist to pull him in close. "Where's your partner?" he asked while thumping a knee into Paul's stomach.

Even though Paul had absorbed the full brunt of Clint's attack, he wasn't about to let go of his pistol. He bent his arm as much as he could toward Clint's head and pulled his trigger again.

The shot may not have come close to hitting Clint, but the sound of it was more than enough to put a powerful

ringing into his ears. Also, the fire from its barrel filled
Clint's vision with a murky cloud that nearly made him
pull away from Paul out of pure instinct. He hung on, however, and was about to take the pistol away from Paul when
another shot was fired. This one didn't come from Paul.

Clint knew better than to anticipate what he would find.
Doing so would limit what he might see. Even so, it took
him a split second to realize that Mose wasn't in that alley
with them. Instead, Mason had been the other man to fire
at him and he was about ready to do so again. Before that
happened, Clint tightened his grip on Paul and twisted his
entire body around.

Paul was nearly taken off his feet by Clint's sudden
movement. He grunted a few surprised words while being
pulled to a spot where he caught the bullet that Mason had
intended for Clint. Hot lead drilled through Paul's back
and erupted from his shoulder to send a bloody spray onto
the side of Clint's face. Paul thrashed in pain from the
impact, which was as good a time as any for Clint to let
him drop.

The other man had barely hit the ground when Clint
searched for Mason. All he found was a wiry man in a
brown suit who was too petrified to move. When he saw
a flicker of motion directly behind the man in the suit,
Clint shouted, "Move!"

Where the man in the suit had been frozen in place
before, he couldn't move fast enough when he heard that
single command. The frightened local got his feet moving
so quickly that they skidded against the dirt without finding enough purchase to carry him anywhere. As he started
falling forward, he dug his boots in and finally managed
to clear the alley.

All of this had taken less than three seconds. In that time, Clint had spotted Mason trying to get into a hat shop across the street. When Mason opened the shop's front door, Clint drew his modified Colt and fired from the hip to put a round into the edge of the door. Wood splinters flew through the air and Mason jumped away as the door was knocked shut by the passing round.

Pivoting on the balls of his feet, Mason fired two shots in quick succession. The first punched into a wall about a foot to Clint's left and the second hissed past Clint's temple. Not wanting to see where a third one would go, Clint threw himself backward to press himself flat against the building behind him. Across the street from him, Mason had ducked behind the best cover he could find, which was a post supporting the awning of the hat shop he'd tried to enter a moment ago.

"You made one hell of a big mistake," Clint shouted. "It's not too late to put things right."

Mason answered that by leaning out to fire a shot toward the alley. There was barely enough time for Clint to find a new place to stand before another bullet punched a hole into the wall a few inches away from him. Each shot was drawing closer to its mark, which meant Mason would draw blood real soon. Instead of waiting for that to happen, Clint brought his Colt up so he could sight along the top of its barrel at Mason.

Exhaling slowly while squeezing the trigger, Clint sent a round blazing through the air. Mason stumbled at that moment, saving his own life when the shot missed by less than an inch, shattering the window behind his target. Voices from within the hat shop rose to a chorus of panicked screams, telling him that there were more than a few customers inside.

"Damn," Clint muttered. He couldn't fire through that window again without taking the risk of hurting or killing someone inside. There wasn't a reason for Mason to know that, however.

Before Mason had a chance to think about much of anything, Clint fired twice. Both shots landed exactly where he'd wanted them to go and they chipped off sizable pieces from the post Mason was using as cover. Both pieces of lead wound up embedded within the post, where they could do no harm to any innocent bystanders. They couldn't do much harm to Mason either, but he didn't sit still long enough to figure that out for himself. Suddenly losing confidence in the post as a protective barrier, Mason hunched down low and ran away from it.

Clint smiled as he watched his hastily conceived plan come to fruition. Now that Mason was running along the street and people were scattering to clear a path for him, Clint just needed to catch up and take him down. His task was made even easier when Mason fired off his remaining shots behind him in an attempt to cover his retreat. Two of those shots drilled into the corner of the building at the mouth of the alley and the last one sailed through empty air.

After taking less than two steps in pursuit of Mason, Clint was stopped by the sound of another pistol's hammer being cocked back.

"Not another step," Mose warned.

Clint slowly turned to get a look behind him. Instinct more than anything else told him that he had enough leeway to do that much at least. Mose stood there, battered from the beating he'd already taken, holding his pistol in a trembling hand.

"You're in over your head," Clint said.

"I told you! Not another . . ." Mose trailed off to form a strained wheeze instead of one more word. His finger clenched around his trigger, but not until his arm had become too heavy for him to lift. The limb dangled uselessly from his shoulder as the gun went off, sending its round into the dirt near his feet. Mose dropped to his knees, then to all fours.

Gigi stood behind him. Her eyes were wide and her dagger was buried as far into Mose's back as it could go. For a second, she appeared to be stunned by what had happened. Then, she reached down to grab the knife handle protruding from between Mose's shoulder blades and leaned all of her weight behind it to drive it in just a bit deeper.

"The other one's getting away," she said.

Clint looked into the street to see Mason rounding the nearest corner. If he ran down to the other end of the alley and made a sharp turn, Clint figured he could catch up to the gunman. Under normal circumstances, he wouldn't have hurried off and left a woman to fend for herself in the middle of a fight. In this case, however, Clint was fairly certain Gigi could handle whatever came her way.

EIGHTEEN

When Clint circled back around to that alley, the only people waiting there for him were a dead body and half a dozen confused locals. The locals milled around, talking to each other and gesturing wildly as if they were describing a stage show they'd just seen. Clint continued moving past them to another group who were also having an animated discussion. This group, however, caught his interest much more than the first.

"Did you see where they went?" asked one man with a long beard and spectacles.

There were three women standing nearby and all of them shivered nervously. One of them said, "I don't want to know where they went. I just want to go home."

"I'd like to know where they went," said the second woman while wriggling in close to a man who was either her husband or suitor, "so I can go the opposite direction."

"You want to know what I think?" the third woman asked.

Clint hurried forward to cut through the group, grab the third woman by the hand, and lead her away. "You should think twice before leaving your family to fend for themselves for supper," he snapped. "And a late supper, no less!"

Since he hadn't jostled any of them on his way through and since the woman was going along with him without much resistance, the rest of the group quickly forgot about Clint and returned to their gossiping.

After taking her another couple of yards, Clint looked to the woman he'd spirited away and snarled, "What the hell is wrong with you, Gigi?"

"I was hiding in plain sight," she replied. "It's not like anyone could convince them nothing had happened. Not after you and those other two charged in like bulls in a china shop."

"Other three, you mean. Two dead and one alive."

After taking a moment to add them up, Gigi nodded. "Right. I forgot about the one that was shot."

"He is dead, right?" Clint asked. "He sure looked that way when I left."

"He's dead."

"Good. Now if we could just get away from here without attracting any attention from the law, I'll be happy."

"I told you not to worry about the law," Gigi assured him.

"The best way to stay alive is to plan for the worst and hope for the best."

She smiled and nodded. "That's good advice. I'll have to pass that along to some of my customers."

"No charge."

"Don't be silly."

After walking down the street and making their way to a short stretch of banks and offices that were locked up for the night, Clint slowed his pace and allowed himself to breathe a little easier. "Where's someplace we can go for a while?" he asked.

"What for? To hide?"

"I'd just like to get off the street for a few hours, but would rather not circle back around to your tent."

"I know someplace that should suit you."

"It needs to suit both of us," he said. "You're not going back to that place until I can check on a few things."

"What are you checking on?" she asked.

Clint tightened his grip on her arm to pull her in close for a few steps. "Could you just take me to this spot you're thinking of instead of asking so many questions?"

"Sure, but it may be a little cramped."

NINETEEN

When Gigi had taken him to the wagon parked on the outskirts of town, Clint had thought she meant for them to
ride out to whatever spot she'd been telling him about.
After unlocking the rear door and stepping inside, however, it became clear that she wasn't planning on going
anywhere else.

Clint stood at the back end of the wagon. "We're not
driving this thing anywhere?" he asked.

Lighting a single lantern and twisting the knob so the
flame was just bright enough to dispel a few shadows, she
replied, "Did you see any horses hitched to it?"

"No."

"Well, that answers that question, doesn't it?"

The wagon was only slightly wider than something that
any family might use to carry their household from one
side of the country to the other. Small trunks lined one
side and the other side was piled high with boxes of different sizes that somehow fit together like a massive

puzzle. Gigi placed the lantern on top of one of the trunks and then turned toward the front of the wagon so she could root through another trunk.

"Do you sleep in here sometimes?" Clint asked.

Without looking back to him, she replied, "No, that's what the house in town is for."

"Considering how much sweet-talking you do for your customers, I'm amazed what a smart mouth you've got."

"You're not a customer."

"That's true. What are you doing?"

Gigi peeled off the first few layers of fabric wrapped around her hips. "Getting out of these rags and into something a bit more practical."

Clint hunched over so he could step into the wagon and shut the little door behind him. "I don't know," he said. "I kind of like those rags."

"Of course you do. Everyone does."

"I'd think the men who visit you would be more partial to them than the women."

"The men like them for obvious reasons," she said while removing all but the last layer covering her lower half. As she unwrapped her upper body, she explained, "Women like them because they make me look like they expect me to look."

"You mean . . . like a gypsy."

"Exactly."

"You look like a gypsy because you are a gypsy." Furrowing his brow, Clint added, "Aren't you?"

"Whatever you prefer."

Clint reached out to steady himself using the stacks on either side of him. The top of the wagon was too low for him to stand completely straight, but he was able to get mostly there once he'd removed his hat. Thanks to the iron hoops functioning as arches above him, he was granted a bit more room than he'd been expecting.

Now that she'd removed her loose-fitting blouse and some of the scarves that had been wrapped around her shoulders and midsection, Clint could see the smooth skin of her back and neck. Squinting into the flickering light thrown off by the lantern, he approached her and placed his fingertip near her shoulder at a spot that was partly covered by her hair. "What's this?" he asked while tapping a black circle that was about the size of a penny.

"The tattoo?"

"Yeah."

"You didn't notice that the last time I was undressed?" she asked.

"I'll admit I was a bit distracted."

"Just a little memory from my youth."

"Is that a gypsy marking?" he asked.

"I'm not really a gypsy," Gigi told him. "I'm Russian."

"Plenty of fortune-tellers put on the whole gypsy act. You certainly pull it off better than most."

"Thank you. I do come by it honestly, though. My grandmother was as gypsy as any woman could get. I'm halfway there myself, but don't have all the blood ties needed to get all the way."

"Close enough to fool me," Clint said. His attention had already been distracted just by watching her. Having removed some simpler clothes from one of the trunks, Gigi stripped out of the rest of the filmy material that had covered her. That left only a wide swath of thin cotton wrapped around her waist and tied on one side to keep it in place.

She took hold of a red blouse with gold embroidering

and was lifting it to slip over her head when she stopped and asked, "What are you doing?"

Clint's hands had started on her back and moved to her sides. "Nothing," he said while easing his hands around to brush the sides of her breasts.

"Doesn't feel like nothing." When he pressed against her so she could feel his erection on her backside, she added, "And neither does that."

Pausing, Clint said, "I'm trying to figure out if that was an insult or not."

"No," she whispered while reaching back to run her fingers through his hair. "It definitely wasn't an insult."

TWENTY

Gigi allowed the clothes she'd gathered to fall from her hands as Clint moved in behind her. She let out a long, contented sigh when he began playing with her nipples and kissing along the side of her neck. When she tried to turn around to face him, however, he tightened his grip just enough to keep her in place.

"I see you have something in mind," she whispered.

Clint answered that by unbuckling his pants and sliding them down. His cock was rigid and he rubbed it against her backside like a promise of things to come. She grabbed on to something on either side for support and let her head fall forward.

"You feel so damn good," she groaned.

Keeping one hand on her breast, Clint slid his other hand down along the front of her body until his fingers moved through the thick patch of downy hair between Gigi's legs. They'd been together only once before, but that was enough time for him to pick up on a few things here and there. One of those things was a particular little spot on her right inner thigh that caused a good portion of her body to quake. He found it in a matter of seconds.

"Jesus," she breathed.

"This wagon is too small," Clint said. "Get down on your knees."

"Anything you say. Just don't stop."

She lowered herself to the floor of the wagon, and Clint did the same. As soon as he was able, his hand found her sensitive spot once again and rubbed a little harder. Before long, he slipped a finger inside her just enough to feel how moist she was. Gigi's pussy was slick and plenty ready for him.

All Clint had to do was move his hard shaft between her thighs and Gigi spread her knees apart a bit more while lifting her backside a little higher. The slope of her ass formed a smooth line down to her back, the sight of which made Clint even harder than he already was. When he slipped inside her, it was like putting out a fire that was about to rage out of anyone's control.

"Oh God," she moaned while grabbing one of the nearby boxes so strongly that she almost pulled the entire stack down onto them both.

Clint reached out with both hands to cup Gigi's breasts again. Her body was just the right length for him to do that while grinding his cock deep into her. She let out an almost animal moan while arching her back. He couldn't help smiling at what he was doing to her. It did Clint some good to drive a woman as crazy as most of them could drive a man at any given time. He savored the moment while putting his hands on her shoulders and pounding into her with powerful thrusts.

Gigi turned to look at him over her shoulder. A few beads of sweat rolled down her face and her mouth hung open without making a sound. She clenched her eyes shut the moment Clint entered her and remained still with every inch of his cock filling her dripping pussy.

For a few seconds, Gigi stretched her arms in front of her like a cat. She lowered her chest to the floor and pressed her palms against the boards at the front of the wagon as she started rocking her body back and forth. Clint reflexively stood still and allowed her to slide him in and out of her.

Now he was the one who was speechless.

Her backside was plump and round as a perfectly ripened fruit. Clint rubbed it as she impaled herself on him again and again. Just when he thought he was about to explode, she pushed herself against him and slowly ground her hips in a slow circle.

His rigid cock was held tight by the muscles between Gigi's thighs. The slightest movement was all she needed to perform in order to drive him out of his mind. Clint gripped her ass in both hands, held her firm, and took back the reins by pumping in and out of her in a rhythm of his choosing.

Suddenly, Gigi straightened her arms so she could prop up the upper portion of her body. Her breath came in quickening gasps, and she tossed her hair straight back while craning her neck. Her climax was powerful and lengthy, ending only when she no longer had the strength to keep herself up on all fours. Before Clint could move within her again, she turned around to face him.

"I told you to stay on all fours," he said.

Smiling, Gigi replied, "Shut up," and pushed him down onto his back. The moment Clint's shoulders hit the floor, she wrapped her lips around his thick penis and began sucking him.

Clint was already feeling damn good, and when she

started running her tongue up and down along his shaft, he knew he wouldn't be able to control himself for long. Reading his movements and groans as well as she could read any spread of Tarot cards, Gigi licked and sucked his cock to drive him straight over the edge.

Every now and then, she drew her lips in tight on him and then took every last inch into her mouth. Then, she allowed him to slip from her mouth so he could only feel her tongue sliding all the way down to the base of his shaft before returning to his tip. Dragging her fingernails along Clint's stomach, she took him into her mouth once more so she could bob her head vigorously up and down.

Clint's heels scraped against the floor and his hands sifted through Gigi's hair. Soon, his hips began to pump and he arched his back as his pleasure built to its boiling point. When she felt him tense, Gigi sucked him harder and faster.

From there, it was only a matter of seconds before he exploded into her mouth. Gigi made a soft humming sound that he could feel all the way down to his toes. Her tongue slipped back and forth against his erection until she'd swallowed every last drop he had to offer. When he was spent, Clint could barely open his eyes.

Gigi climbed to her feet and looked down at Clint in much the same way a she-wolf watched a deer that it had just crippled. "You're full of surprises, Adams."

"I could say the same about you," Clint replied once he had enough breath in his lungs.

"If it's all the same to you, I should probably get dressed."

Since he barely had the energy to lift his head, Clint told her, "Sure. Go on and do that."

TWENTY-ONE

"Where are you going?" Gigi whispered in the darkness.

Several hours had passed since she'd gotten dressed, undressed, and then dressed again. She and Clint had lined the floor of the wagon with thick blankets, making it comfortable enough to lie down there. It was time to leave, however, and Clint had barely unlatched the little door at the back of the wagon when he'd been discovered.

"I'm taking a stroll," he replied. "Go back to sleep."

"I wasn't asleep. Neither were you."

"Then it's about time you got some rest."

She came at him from the back of the wagon so quickly that the entire thing rattled with the impact of her feet. "Don't presume to tell me what I can or can't do, especially when we're inside my wagon!"

"That's perfect," Clint said as he stepped outside. "Because I am no longer in your wagon. I suggest you stay there and wait for me to come back."

"Why?"

"Fine, then. Do what you please. Get yourself killed."

Although she stepped to the very edge of the wagon's little doorway, Gigi didn't set foot outside. "You think I may get killed?"

"I think you're being watched by killers. Killers, I might add, that you've already upset. I'd say that puts you in a pot of hot water."

"You're going back to my house?" she asked.

"You really are talented. Now get back inside and wait for me to come back."

Gigi pulled herself into the wagon and shut the door. Before Clint could take a full three steps away from that wagon, she opened the door again and announced, "I'm staying here because it's the smart thing to do—*not* because you told me to do it."

Without breaking his stride, Clint said, "You really put me in my place. Well played."

He didn't have to see her to imagine the expression on her face when she shut the wagon's door again.

Clint made his way across town, confident that Gigi would know better than to try and follow. She could very well sneak around behind him, but she would have the good sense to give him a wide berth for the time being.

He wasn't even halfway to the spot where the fish vendor and Madame Giselle's place shared an alleyway when Clint could hear commotion from that street. Apparently, those carts didn't close down at normal business hours. In fact, once he got close enough to see that stretch of property for himself, Clint was certain there was a whole new category of things being sold there.

As he walked along with his hat pulled down to cover a good portion of his face, Clint could feel the tension coming from those around him. Men watched him to make certain he would pass them by without causing any trouble. Transactions were being made that were obviously not meant for prying eyes. Clint's imagination ran wild with the possibilities existing in such a place.

Every breath he took was tainted by smoke that would make his head spin if he drew in too much. The spot where he'd purchased his meat on a stick was now occupied by a man who was older than the hills and selling something that he kept mostly concealed beneath a blanket. Judging by the movement beneath that tarp, Clint didn't even want to know what the old man was showing his customer.

Clint continued walking at a pace that wasn't going to draw any undue attention his way. Anyone walking down that street, whether they had business there or not, was surely going to be spotted. The trick was not to look overly bothered by it. Clint didn't look directly at anyone, but didn't look away either. All the while, he searched the faces of local denizens for one or two familiar ones. It wasn't an easy task for a man with only one set of eyes.

Having made it all the way to the fish vendor's cart, Clint took a quick look toward the tent bearing Madame Giselle's name. The only living thing he spotted was a mangy cat sniffing around one of the vendor's crates that had been left beside the cart.

As much as Clint wanted to investigate a bit closer, he knew better than to be so obvious. After everything he'd seen and heard, he would have bet a small fortune on the fact that someone was nearby keeping an eye on that place at any time. He just hoped anyone doing that job at the moment was tired, distracted, or both. Considering the thick stench of opium drifting through the air, there was an even better chance that someone staying put for too long was too far out of their own skull to notice Clint anyway.

Despite all that, he took the more cautious route by passing that alley altogether and pretending to be interested in whatever was being sold from the back of a cart that still bore fresh bullet holes in its side. After looking over the shoulder of a man who plainly didn't want him there, Clint moved along. As far as he could tell, there wasn't anyone following him.

There were only slightly fewer people in the merchant district at that time of night, but they were conducting their business much more quietly than during the daylight hours. Clint drifted from vendor to vendor, collecting one nasty scowl after another. Finally, he made it to the alley that allowed him to get to the house where Gigi conducted her business.

When he approached from the other end of the alley, Gigi's house was the first place he spotted. He almost didn't recognize it since he couldn't see the tent attached to it right away. Clint kept his head down and his hands in his pocket to present the smallest silhouette possible for anyone who might be looking at him. Considering how disinterested everyone seemed to be in him, Clint felt like he was putting on a performance for a theater full of empty seats.

Clint stayed still for a few moments. As he watched the house, he meandered slowly toward a thick cluster of shadows nearby. By the time he brushed a shoulder against a wall, he felt as if he was almost completely invisible.

"So," said someone that Clint couldn't see, "are you going to keep circling the place like a vulture or are you going to come in?"

TWENTY-TWO

Clint's hand twitched toward the Colt at his side as his eyes searched for the source of the voice he'd just heard. Even when he spotted the shadow in the entrance to Gigi's tent, he wasn't completely certain it was anything at all.

"Well, come on," the shadow said as it waved at him. "Might as well get yourself in here."

Clint felt like a fool for not seeing the man in the tent, especially since he'd been looking in that exact spot for a sign of trouble. Now that he was granted a good look at the man who'd been waiting there, Clint could see the badge pinned to the man's shirt. The shadow disappeared inside the tent, so Clint stayed quiet as he followed it inside.

"You move like a damn cat," Clint said after he'd ducked through the tent flap. "It's a mite disconcerting."

Sheriff Wheeler had one hand in his pocket. The other was idly tapping one of the mystical books situated on a table nearby. Half of his black coat was hooked around his holster in what was most certainly not an accidental fashion.

"It helps to walk lightly around here," he said. "Especially at this time of night."

Before Clint could wonder if they were truly alone inside the tent, he saw Patrick stick his nose out from the next room. After getting a curt nod from Clint, the tent's lone guardian went back into the main room and waited.

"What brings you here?" Clint asked.

"I should be the one asking you that," Wheeler replied. "This is my town, after all."

"But not your tent. At least, not as far as I know."

"Not yours either, if I'm not mistaken."

"I'm friendly with the owner."

"Yes," Wheeler replied in a smug tone. "So I've heard. How do you know Miss Pietrov?"

"We go back a ways," Clint said.

"Are you on familiar terms with a man by the name of Wilhelm Torquelan?"

"Not as such, but I'm looking to change that."

The lawman's eyebrows lifted a bit. "Are you, now? Looking for employment?"

"No," Clint said. "Just looking for him."

"For what purpose?"

"For the purpose of asking why the hell he wanted to kill me. Actually, I have a pretty good idea of why. I'd still like to hear it from him, though."

The sheriff's pale face looked much more comfortable in dim lighting. At least he didn't look so much like something that had been left out too long to bake in the sun. His eyes narrowed with a lawman's suspicion, and his mouth was completely lost beneath his brushy mustache. "And once you see him, I imagine you'd want to kill him for sending those men after you."

Clint shrugged and walked around the small space enclosed by the tent's canvas walls. "Normally, after one man tries to kill another, their next meeting doesn't turn out well."

"Not for one of them, that's for certain."

"But you were expecting trouble," Clint pointed out. "Or am I supposed to believe you just like to spend time in this tent at the wee hours of the night?"

"I'm always expecting trouble," Wheeler told him. "That's what I get paid for. And you, Mr. Adams, are trouble."

"Me? I'm no outlaw."

"I didn't call you an outlaw. You're trouble."

"Seems you've heard a thing or two about me," Clint said. "Probably nothing more than rumor and wild talk from a bunch of drunks."

Sheriff Wheeler stood so he could see Clint and both doors leading from the tent. Hooking his thumbs over his gun belt, he said, "I've heard that you're the sort of man who comes to a quiet town and doesn't leave until there's been blood spilled in the streets. Whatever happens to put that blood there may not be your fault exactly, but it wouldn't have been spilled if you hadn't shown up in the first place."

"All I came here for was a drink and to cool my heels before moving along."

"I'd say that falls in line with what I just said."

"I suppose it does," Clint admitted with a shrug. "What would you have me do when someone takes a shot at me? Shake the other man's hand and let him be on his way?"

"That would help men like me perform their duties much easier, but no. I wouldn't expect that of someone."

"Speaking of expectations," Clint said. "I would expect a lawman in this town to keep a tight rein on a street like this one. I see, despite some things I've heard about you from a few of the locals, that you do a fairly good job of that."

"A fairly good job?" Wheeler sneered. "I got the drop on you, didn't I?"

"Fair enough."

"And who's been saying unfavorable things about me?"

"Doesn't matter."

Scowling, Wheeler said, "It was that gypsy woman, wasn't it?"

From the corner of his eye, Clint could see Patrick doing his best to stay hidden while keeping watch on what was going on in the rest of the tent.

Since Clint wasn't about to answer that question, Wheeler tried his luck with another one. "What did she say about me?" the lawman asked.

"I never said it was her!"

"Then what did anyone say?"

Exasperated, Clint said, "That you're a useless lump of a man."

Wheeler looked as though he'd just been stricken by a kick below his belt. "Useless?"

Clint shrugged. "You asked and wouldn't let up. If it helps you feel any better, I can see that's not a fair assessment of you."

According to the sour look on Wheeler's face, it didn't help him feel better at all. Then again, it was the same sour expression the lawman had worn since the first time Clint had ever seen him. Whatever aggravation the lawman was harboring, he swallowed it down like the bitter pill it was. "I figured someone would be coming along sooner or later. That's why I waited here."

"You were expecting me?"

"If not you, another one of Torquelan's men. Now that he's lost a few of those men, retaliation is inevitable."

"He lost a few men?" Clint asked.

Wheeler's expression became even more sour. "Are you really going to tell me you had nothing to do with that?"

Clint's poker face might as well have been cut from bedrock.

"Or that you didn't even know about it?" Wheeler added.

"I guess I did hear a thing or two along those lines," Clint said.

"Then I'll ask you up front. Did you have anything to do with that?"

"With those men being shot?"

"Of course."

Clint took a breath and started to speak when he was stopped by a swiftly raised finger.

"Fair warning," Wheeler said. "If you ask if I'm talking about Torquelan's men just to buy yourself some time, I'll toss you into jail on principle."

"In that case," Clint replied, "yes. I did have something to do with that."

"Even the one who was stabbed in the back? That doesn't strike me as your method."

Clint made a mental note to watch his step when around the lawman. He'd underestimated him once before and doing so again could very well be a costly mistake. "I didn't stab that man in the back, Sheriff. Whoever did was a concerned citizen trying to keep me from getting killed by one of those assholes Torquelan sent. That's all I aim to say on the matter."

Wheeler studied Clint carefully and nodded. "I can respect that, Mr. Adams. The last thing I want to do in my town is discourage my citizens from being concerned. Las Primas is better off without that fellow."

"And the others?"

"If you have to ask that question," Wheeler said with a smile that seemed more than a little uncomfortable beneath all those whiskers, "then you obviously never had a chat with them."

"I suppose so. Well then, I guess I'll be leaving."

"What's the hurry?"

"I've got business to tend to," Clint said.

"Business with Torquelan?"

"That's right."

"Do you even know where to find him?" the lawman asked.

"Actually, I was hoping to find another of his gunmen and then get him to take me there."

"Or I could point you in the right direction. Could be a lot less messy."

"Maybe," Clint said. "Maybe not."

TWENTY-THREE

Clint didn't for one moment consider that Wheeler would simply point him in the right direction where Torquelan was concerned. And as was the case with most of the instances where Clint was being pessimistic, he was proven correct. The sheriff walked along with him down one street and up another without saying a word as to where their final destination might be.

"Where are the rest of your men?" Clint asked.

"How many were you expecting?" the sheriff replied.

"I don't know. At least a deputy or two."

"I thought you weren't intending on starting any big amount of trouble."

Rather than play along with the sheriff's game of words, Clint let out a heavy sigh and kept walking.

Before too long, Sheriff Wheeler said, "It's probably best for us to keep our numbers down. At least, this time around."

"And if there is trouble?" Clint asked. "Not that I would dream of starting anything, mind you."

"I've got three deputies at my disposal. Only one of them is good for much of anything apart from holding a gun while wearing a purposeful look on his face. If there was trouble with Mr. Torquelan, all of those men wouldn't do us much good if they were along."

Clint was surprised with that amount of honesty from the lawman. Whether it was given to him out of respect or just to staunch the flow of questions, he decided to honor the gesture by making the rest of the walk in silence.

When they came to a stop, it was in front of a strip of three buildings that had two floors each. Clint first thought that the sheriff meant to question him or point something out. When the lawman didn't seem to be going or doing anything else, Clint asked, "Is this it?"

"If you were expecting dancing girls, I can recommend a saloon or two," Wheeler replied. "If you're after Wilhelm Torquelan, this is the place."

"Which one?"

"All three. It's sort of a compound."

"Doesn't look like anyone's home."

"Then there's no reason to knock." With that, the lawman walked toward a narrow alley along the left side of the row of buildings.

As Clint followed him, his hand instinctually came to a rest upon the Colt at his side. His eyes wandered up and down along the front and then side of the building, finding nothing that seemed out of the ordinary. In fact, if he'd been walking down the street on his own, he would have written off those buildings as being abandoned. It wasn't until they were about to circle around to the rear of the buildings that he caught sight of one flicker of light in a sliver of one window.

Squinting up at that window, Clint could see the light was constant and wavering. Then he could tell it was just a lantern or candle in that room, but the window itself had been covered by something. As far as he could tell, all the windows were covered by something and it was just that one's covering that had slipped enough to allow some hint of light to get through. It was a simple trick for people to give themselves privacy. Oftentimes, though, the simplest tricks were also the most effective.

"How many men does he have working for him?" Clint asked.

"No more than five or six at a time. That was last time I checked."

"And how long ago was that?"

Wheeler shrugged. "Been a while."

"How many are in there now?"

"That's what I aim to find out." Without another word, Sheriff Wheeler put boot to door and stormed inside.

TWENTY-FOUR

"All right, then," Clint said as he tightened his grip on his modified Colt. "Here we go."

Sheriff Wheeler had already announced his presence in a booming voice that rolled through the dimly lit building along with the echo of the door being kicked in. There were only a few lanterns hanging here and there, providing just enough light for Clint to keep from walking into a wall. His eyes quickly adjusted to the shadows, however, and none too soon. Some of the men that had already been inside that building were coming to answer the lawman's call.

"Wilhelm Torquelan!" Wheeler bellowed. "This is the sheriff! Come down here right now!"

The first man that Clint saw was a stout fellow with a thin mustache and a sharp chin. He filled the far end of a hallway, taking a moment to get a look at the men who'd entered the building.

"Where's Torquelan?" Wheeler asked.

The man didn't move and didn't say a word. Even so, Clint knew there was going to be trouble. Narrowing his eyes into slits, the man drew his pistol and took aim. He got a shot off, but not before two other rounds were sent down that hallway.

The first round came from Wheeler, who'd pulled his trigger as fast as he could. The second came from Clint. While slightly slower than the lawman's shot, Clint took an extra fraction of a second to fire properly. That bullet clipped the gunman's hip and sent him spinning on one foot like a top.

"You there!" Wheeler hollered. "I see you hiding. Come out and show me your hands."

Clint hadn't spotted the man Wheeler had found. When that one stepped out where he could be seen, there was another directly behind him. He couldn't make out any details on either man's face, but Clint could see the barrel of a shotgun, which was all he needed to set him on his course of action.

Stepping forward, Clint shoved Wheeler to one side while straightening his arm so he could sight along the Colt's barrel.

He didn't pull his trigger right away.

Clint knew he already had the drop on the man with the shotgun, but he was more than willing to give him a chance to save his own hide. Rather than put a bullet through him as quickly as possible, Clint waited for a heartbeat. When the lead was already flying, that was an eternity.

Everything Clint needed to see was written on the shotgunner's face. The other man's eyes were fixed on a target and his hands gripped the shotgun with purpose. All the way down to the marrow in Clint's bones, he knew the man was going to fire that scattergun. That left only one alternative.

The Colt in Clint's hand barked once, spitting its round through the air. He knew exactly where it would land before it got there and watched as blood sprayed from the other man's shoulder. The impact of that round spun the shotgunner toward the wall. Instead of pulling his triggers out of reflex, he grunted and brought the shotgun back around to point at the sheriff and Clint.

Clint fired once more, swearing under his breath as a bullet through the skull sent the shotgunner straight to hell.

The next shot that was fired came from less than a foot away from where Clint was standing. Reflexively, Clint dropped to one knee and pivoted toward the gunshot. Sheriff Wheeler stood his ground, smoking pistol in hand, staring at a doorway that Clint hadn't even seen in the dimly lit corridor.

"He get you?" Wheeler asked.

Clint stood back up and looked through the doorway, which had been cut directly into the wall without benefit of a frame. There wasn't a handle on the outside of it either, which had made it blend in perfectly with the wall until it had been opened. The man who'd opened it was sprawled upon the floor with a fresh wound in his chest. The gun he'd been carrying was discarded and his feet kicked through the last tantrums of his murderous life.

"No," Clint replied. "He didn't get me. Didn't even see the son of a bitch."

"I heard this place was tricky."

"Tricky as in secret doors?" Clint asked.

"Something like that."

"Could've warned me."

"Actually, I didn't believe them rumors to be true," Wheeler replied.

"What about now? Anything else you want to tell me?"

Wheeler shrugged. "That bastard nearly got me, too! What the hell else do you want from me?"

Clint let out a weary sigh while reloading the Colt. As they continued down the hallway, he was sure to keep the lawman where he could keep his eye on him. Every step of the way, he became less comfortable with the situation. Meeting an enemy on their ground was never a great idea. Wading in even deeper after that enemy had already tried to kill you was even worse.

"Wait," Clint said as he stopped in his tracks.

The sheriff became fidgety the instant he was no longer moving. "What is it? What do you see?"

"You keep going that way," he said while nodding down the hall. "I'm doubling back." When Wheeler looked at him angrily, Clint motioned toward the previously hidden doorway. Fortunately, the lawman picked up on the idea of not announcing their true intentions for anyone to hear. He didn't seem to be thrilled about Clint's plan, but he was willing to go along with it for the moment.

Shifting to movements that didn't make so much noise, Clint backtracked the short distance to the door and took a quick peek into the next room. The man Wheeler had gunned down was on his back, staring up into oblivion. Other than that, there wasn't much else to see. The room was slightly larger than a closet and, as near as Clint could figure, was designed especially for the purpose of ambushing anyone in the hallway. As Clint stepped over the body of the would-be assassin, a chill ran down his back.

That room stank of death and plenty of it. This wasn't the first time the trap had been sprung. The men behind it knew what they were doing when it came to killing. If Clint had anything to say about it, they wouldn't be doing it much longer.

TWENTY-FIVE

Sheriff Wheeler kept his eyes pointed forward as he approached the first man Clint had shot through the hip. "Where'd the other one go?" he whispered.

The wounded gunman had been trying to get back to his feet, but only one of his legs was working properly. The other was bleeding and would probably come back after a whole lot of healing, but not tonight. Glaring up at the lawman, he snarled, "Up yer ass!"

Stooping down, Wheeler reached out with one hand to pick up the shotgun that had been dropped by the gunman's deceased partner. "You want to wind up like this man right here beside you? Keep right on talking that way."

No matter how much the gunman wanted to keep up his tough demeanor, he couldn't help looking over at the dead man on the floor not too far away.

"I'm playing my hand right now," Wheeler said. He didn't exactly point his gun directly at the other man's head, but he made it real clear the pistol was ready to be

used again. "Since you and these idiot friends of yours
already fired on me, anything I do from here on out is in
self-defense. Anything."

The cold intent of the lawman's words didn't go unno-
ticed. Something from deeper within the building was
slammed against a wall and the sound hit the wounded
man like a slap in the face. "There's another door," he said.
"Straight behind me."

Wheeler looked into the next room, which was empty
apart from a single chair that was almost too rotten to support the weight of the lantern sitting on it. "Room's empty."

"That's where he went."

"Another trap door?"

The wounded man nodded. "Just walk straight back
and push on the wall. It'll open."

"What's waiting for me on the other side?" Wheeler
asked.

"How the hell would I know? I'm sitting here, ain't I?"

"If you're setting me up to get shot at again, you'll be
laying there. Right beside that poor soul."

The gunman didn't say anything. He didn't have to. He
was too rattled to tell any kind of lie. Since he knew that
was the best he could hope for, Sheriff Wheeler pressed on.

Clint took his time moving through the hidden room. It only
took a few steps, but each one of them could very well have
been his last. When he made it to the door on the other side,
he glanced out to find a darkened hallway. The shadows
were plenty thick, but not thick enough to hide anything
more than a mouse. Keeping his head down, he moved
swiftly toward the sound of approaching footsteps.

The door Clint used led into another cramped hall that

went for about three paces before angling ninety degrees to the left. Whoever was rounding that corner coming toward him was moving with the confidence of someone who knew they couldn't be seen. Clint showed him the problem with that train of thought by attacking him the instant he stepped into view.

First, Clint saw the dull shine of polished iron. The man coming down that hall already had his gun drawn and was holding it in front of him as he rounded the corner. Next, Clint dropped his left hand down to grab the pistol from along the top of its barrel. Before the man holding the gun realized what was happening, Clint twisted the pistol until he heard the snap of a breaking trigger finger.

The man that Clint had surprised had a face smeared with coal dust and smelled as if he'd just climbed out of a mine shaft. His eyes were wide with surprise and his mouth opened to let out a snarling obscenity. Clint's hands were full, so he rammed his shoulder into the man's chest and shoved him into a wall.

"Don't move," Clint said.

The twisting corridor must have been close to the main hallway because Clint could hear Sheriff Wheeler's voice. He couldn't make out what the lawman was saying, but he seemed to have things well enough in hand for the moment. When the man against the wall tried to stir, Clint jammed the Colt's barrel into his belly to make him think better of it.

The man stayed still. He even held his breath to keep from making another sound.

Whatever conversation the sheriff was having didn't last much longer. Soon, Wheeler and the man he'd been talking to started walking. "Where are they going?" Clint asked the man directly in front of him.

"How the hell should I know?" the man snarled.

"You know this building. You know where people might go. Tell me where they're going."

"Go see for yourself."

Clint shrugged. "Well then. I suppose that makes you pretty damn useless." All he had to do from there was put a little more pressure behind the pistol that was already wedged into the other man's gut.

"The stairs," the man said in a quick exhale.

"What stairs?"

"There's stairs to the second floor. If they're not walking toward the door leading outside, that's where they're going."

"What about the third floor?" Clint asked.

"Ain't nothing up there but a few spots for men to look down with rifles. This time of night, there's no reason for that."

"I suppose I should be thankful for that, huh?"

The gunman rolled his eyes.

Since the next sounds Clint heard were feet clomping on stairs, he removed the gun barrel from the man's belly. "Take me to the stairs," Clint demanded.

"You're makin' a real big mistake," the gunman warned.

Clint pulled him away from the wall as if he was peeling off a strip of paper. "Since it's too late to take this mistake back, I might as well keep on with it. Besides, I'm curious to see where this one takes me."

TWENTY-SIX

After taking Clint to the stairs, the gunman who'd been knocked around dragged his feet like a kid on his way to a long day of church. Although it would have been simpler to knock the man on the back of the head and leave him lying somewhere, Clint kept him around as a kind of lookout. He didn't expect to be informed if anyone else was about to try to ambush them, but he was confident that he could read any changes in the man's tired face if something was about to happen.

They made it to the second floor without incident. Up there was a short hallway with two rooms on either side. None of them had closed doors and only one had a light flickering inside. When Clint got to the occupied room, Sheriff Wheeler and two other men were there waiting for him.

One of those other men was dressed similar to the others that had been downstairs to greet them. Simple clothes that appeared to be rumpled as if after a long day's ride were wrapped around bodies that were in dire need of a bath. The second man had a full head of salt-and-pepper hair with a mustache to match it and wore a nicely cut brown suit. While it wasn't quite as common as a suit that might be worn by a bank teller, it would have been perfectly fine for the manager of that same bank.

"I see you men did a fine job of keeping the first floor secure," the man in the bank manager's suit said. "You can go."

Even though they'd been dragged upstairs by the scruffs of their necks, neither of the two gunmen Clint and Wheeler had captured seemed to notice them any longer. The man with Wheeler was nursing a wounded leg and he gimped from the room like a scalded dog. The man who'd brought Clint to the stairs asked, "Wh-where should we go, sir?"

"I don't give a damn so long as it's out of my sight."

The man skulked away with his head hung low.

Straightening the lapels of his jacket, the man with the black-and-gray hair said, "Come now, Sheriff. Aren't you going to introduce me to your associate?"

"Clint Adams," Wheeler announced, "this is Wilhelm Torquelan."

The Colt was still in Clint's hand, but Torquelan didn't seem to mind one bit. In fact, he barely even seemed to notice there was a gun pointed at him at all. That told Clint a hell of a lot about the man. Holstering the weapon, Clint extended his hand and said, "Good to meet you. I've already made the acquaintance of some of your associates."

"Yes," Torquelan mused. "From what I heard of the commotion downstairs, I'll be cleaning up the mess for some time."

"Something tells me you have workers to do that sort of thing for you."

"Indeed." Torquelan then shifted his eyes to Wheeler. "At least I won't have to go through the trouble of informing the law as to what transpired here."

"Not at all," Wheeler said. "But there are a few things you can tell me."

Torquelan's office was simple. It was so simple, in fact, that Clint doubted it was a spot the man would spend very much time in at all. There was a desk, a few uncomfortable-looking chairs, and a small safe against one wall. Circling around the desk, Torquelan sat down with his back to a window that was covered by a dark sheet. "Have a seat."

Hurried footsteps rushed down the hall, announcing the arrival of two more gunmen. They huffed with the effort of their run and immediately pointed their guns at Clint and Wheeler. "They killed two and wounded another," one of the men announced.

"And you're too late to do anything about it," Torquelan said. "Get out of my sight."

The men disappeared almost as quickly as they'd arrived.

"Where were we?" Torquelan asked in an overly formal tone.

"I was about to ask you what you knew about three men who've gone missing," Wheeler said.

When Torquelan replied to that question, he did so with a voice dripping with feigned innocence. If he was a woman, he would have batted his eyelashes while saying, "Three men? Why would I know anything about three men who've gone missing?"

"Because they're miners," Wheeler said, obviously not buying Torquelan's act for a moment. "Two had gold claims that were starting to pan out and another had uncovered a vein of silver."

"I hate to say it, but men with that kind of good fortune will have plenty of others gunning for them."

"You made an offer to buy them out."

"Are you sure about that?"

Having remained on his feet after being told to sit, Wheeler stepped closer to the desk and leaned forward to place his hands upon the rough wooden surface. "I spoke to two others who accepted similar offers from you. They told me two of them other three were at the same meeting."

Somehow, Torquelan maintained his innocent façade as he shrugged. Clint had to admire someone who could keep a poker face like that.

"I meet with plenty of miners, Sheriff," Torquelan said. "That's the business I'm in."

"Bullshit," Clint snapped.

Furrowing his brow, Torquelan fixed a glare onto Clint as he said, "Excuse me?"

Clint hadn't moved from his spot, which meant everyone else in the room was in his field of vision. That included the man with the chiseled features dressed in an immaculate, freshly starched suit who stood just outside the doorway Clint had used when coming into the office.

"I said this is a bunch of bullshit," Clint replied. "You sit there acting like a wide-eyed daisy when the stink of gun smoke is still in the air. Maybe the two of you are willing to forget that we were shot at as soon as we set foot in here, but I'm not!"

"And perhaps you've forgotten that when you set foot onto my property," Torquelan said, "you did so by kicking down my door like a common invader. For all I knew, the two of you meant to slaughter me and my men without provocation."

"There's plenty of provocation," Wheeler said. "Just ask the families of those miners you've killed."

"First they were missing and now they're dead?" Torquelan scoffed. "You should at least get your story straight before you do something like this, Sheriff. Judging by the expression on Mr. Adams's face, I'd say he doesn't know anything about this."

"I know your men have been following me since I got to town," Clint said. "And before you try to tell me you don't know about that, I'll have you know I heard it from more than one source."

Torquelan settled into his chair. "I don't suppose you'd name that source?"

"Sure, but I don't have to. You already know I'm speaking the truth."

After a brief pause, Torquelan folded his hands on the desk in front of him. "It seems I owe you an apology, Adams. You've stumbled into an unfortunate situation. If you'd like to wash your hands of the entire matter, I'd be happy to oblige."

"You would, huh? How so?" Clint asked.

"By offering to reimburse you for any losses you may have suffered while in Las Primas and assuring that you will be allowed to leave town without another unfortunate incident befalling you."

"What a generous offer. How long do I have to think it over?"

Torquelan got to his feet. "I assume you won't need much time at all."

"Tell me something," Clint said. "What has all this trouble got to do with Madame Giselle?"

"Madame who?" Torquelan asked. But his poker face

wasn't as good as Clint had originally thought. Despite the
innocence that remained in his voice when he said those
words, Torquelan's eyes showed a subtle twitch in the cor-
ners. It was a twitch that could only be put there by someone
with a particular knack for getting under a man's skin. More
often than not, that someone was of the female variety.

"Madame Giselle," Sheriff Wheeler said. "She's a
fortune-teller in the Cart and Tent District."

"You two may have heard of her, but I haven't,"
Torquelan said. "I have much better ways to spend my time
and money than by handing both over to some gypsy
wrapped in cheap silk." He then motioned toward the door,
where the handsome man was waiting. "Tonight's scuffle
was unfortunate all around."

"That's putting it mildly," Clint said.

"You men came in like brutes," Torquelan continued,
"and mine opened fire like common outlaws. Neither side
has much in the way of redeeming qualities, so I'm willing to let it pass."

Before Clint could mutter the next smart comment that
came to mind, Wheeler said, "I can abide by that. Of
course, I'd like to have a chance to speak to you again.
How about tomorrow? That should give us all a chance to
cool our heels."

"That would be splendid . . . if I didn't have business
that takes me out of town tomorrow. Why don't we have
our next chat when I return?" Torquelan offered. "Until
then, Mr. Darrow will show you out."

With that, Darrow stepped into the room and extended
an arm to reveal the pistols holstered under both shoulders
beneath his jacket. "This way, gentlemen," he said in a
smooth voice.

When Darrow attempted to give Wheeler a nudge toward the door, the lawman turned to him and snarled, "Put a hand on me and you'll pull back a stump."

"I'll have to agree with our host," Clint said. "There's been more than enough excitement for one night." He then led the sheriff out of the building.

TWENTY-SEVEN

Once outside, Clint gave Wheeler a shove toward the street. The sheriff wasted no time at all before spinning around to face him angrily.

"What I said to Darrow goes for you as well, Adams!"

"Funny how you lead me into an ambush without telling me much of anything beforehand and you're the one who's riled up."

Bringing his glare down to a simmer, Wheeler pointed himself toward the corner leading back to the busier part of town and started walking. "I suppose you do have reason to be perturbed."

"Perturbed?" Clint chuckled as he fell into step alongside the sheriff. "I would describe it more as pissed as all hell."

"Say what you like."

"All right, then. After what you pulled, I should knock you onto your ass!"

Wheeler stopped, faced Clint, and placed his hand upon the pistol at his side. "You may have earned some slack with me, but don't you forget who you're speaking to. I'm a duly appointed lawman and you'll respect that."

"I can respect the badge if not the man."

Letting out a measured breath, Wheeler conceded the point with a nod. "I suppose I had that coming."

"That and more as far as I'm concerned. Where are you going?"

Wheeler had resumed his stride down the street and didn't break it when he said, "Home. It's been a long day."

"Do you intend on telling me what the hell this was about?"

"I wasn't going to ask why you were skulking about or what you intended on doing when you got what you were after."

"Yes you did!"

After thinking that over for a moment, Wheeler said, "So I did. If you want to take Torquelan up on his offer to wash your hands of this mess, I don't blame you."

"All I want," Clint said, "is to find out exactly what the hell this mess is!"

Wheeler put his hands on his hips and looked down the street as if he'd just been dropped there from a great height. "I could go for a drink. How about you, Adams?"

"You buying?"

"Sure."

"Then I'm drinking."

They wound up back in the spot Clint had first visited upon entering Las Primas. Sweet Caroline's Spirits was alive and jumping with rowdy music being played by two men strumming banjos. Their feet stomped the floorboards and customers showed their appreciation with a chorus of drunken yells that vaguely resembled singing. Clint and

Wheeler took their beers to a table as far away from the commotion as possible, which didn't do much to lessen the noise blaring through their heads.

"I misjudged you, Adams," Wheeler said. "I've heard plenty about the men you killed and didn't think too highly of it."

"That's not the sort of thing plenty of men would admire," Clint admitted. "Especially lawmen."

"Yes, well, I had you pegged for a common gunman. Maybe even a gunman on Torquelan's payroll."

"So you invited me in there to see what I'd do once I got around those men?"

"And if I didn't like what I saw, I'd put you down."

"Just like that, huh?" Clint asked.

Wheeler nodded and sipped his beer. "That's what the good people of this town pay me to do."

"I suppose it is. So what do you think after what happened back there?"

"I think I'd be plenty able to tell whether you were trying to pull one over on me and I don't believe you were. As for the rest, it seems Mr. Torquelan has got more up his sleeve than I thought."

"You mind telling me about it?"

After another drink, Wheeler seemed much more at ease. Not drunk, but just allowing himself to relax a bit. "Things around here have always been tense where Torquelan is concerned. I've usually been able to keep it under control enough to maintain a certain level of peace in Las Primas."

"It seems Torquelan has plenty of business outside of town," Clint pointed out.

"Which is outside my jurisdiction." Where most lawmen Clint had encountered would let the matter drop right there,

Wheeler added, "It's come to my attention that he's respon-
sible for harming citizens, though, which extends my juris-
dictional boundaries as far as I'm concerned."

"You're talking about those miners?"

"That's right."

"So what's the story with them?" Clint asked.

Wheeler drew a deep breath and shook his head slowly.
"You've already been dragged through enough of this
town's mud. I wouldn't blame you at all if you'd rather just
put this place behind you. Lord knows I've considered it
more than once."

"I'm in this and it's not too hard to see that there's a lot
more beneath the surface. Besides, Torquelan didn't strike
me as the sort of man who'd honor his word by letting me
ride on out of here without incident."

"I'd have to agree with you on that. How familiar are
you with Torquelan's line of work?"

"I've just heard he invests in mining claims."

"Collects them is more like it," Wheeler said. "He offers
to buy them out, and when he's refused, things get ugly."

"Nobody's tried to put him away for stealing property
rights or threatening honest miners?"

"They would, but he's not careless enough to be arrested
that way. He covers his tracks real well."

"Yeah," Clint groaned as he drank some beer. "Snakes
tend to be like that."

"I may have been wrong about you, Adams, but I'm not
wrong about him. Torquelan is a killer and a liar. He's not
a thief, however, which troubles me."

"Why? Because you'd rather deal with a thief?"

"No," Wheeler said. "Because it seems that he's been
collecting a lot more gold mines lately and not by the usual

means. He intimidates miners, buys them off, kills them, cheats them, but outright stealing from them is . . ."

Since Wheeler seemed to be searching for his next words, Clint offered some of his own. "Simple theft is beneath him?"

"That's right. I'm sure he's done it in the past, but he's beyond that now. He doesn't need to steal. Torquelan sees to it that he acquires whatever he wants by eliminating whoever is in possession of it at the time. Simply calling him a thief would be like calling attention to the rain that comes on either side of a tornado. Does that make sense?"

"Not entirely," Clint said with a tired laugh, "but I get the point. What is it that troubles you now as opposed to what's troubled you before?"

"Three miners turned up missing. In the last week, they were declared lost. Torquelan made offers on their claims, but only after their grieving families gave up hope of finding them. Before that, Torquelan has been sending workers to start digging into four more properties he'd bought interests in."

"Controlling interest?"

Wheeler shook his head. "He's taking on partners. That's not strange in itself, but reaching out to invest in so many claims at once isn't like him. And none of those claims I mentioned belong to the miners that went missing. The fact that I discovered all of these happenings at once leads me to believe there's a lot more going on that I haven't found."

"And one of those things you haven't found yet is what Torquelan is doing with those claims from the missing miners."

"That's right," Wheeler said. "Because he's got to be doing something about them. When I looked into it some time ago, I lost one of my deputies."

"Torquelan had him killed?" Clint guessed.

"Worse. He hired him. His name's Mason. I believe you've already met him."

"He was one of your deputies? I never would have guessed that."

"Mason never was a saint," Wheeler said. "Honestly, I was glad to be rid of him. But having him sign on with Torquelan's bunch just when I got close to finding out what was happening with those claims is too much of a coincidence for my liking."

"I'm guessing those claims are fairly lucrative."

Leaning forward, the sheriff dropped his voice to something close to a whisper. "That's just the thing. They were barely starting to produce anything at all. Normally, they'd be way below Torquelan's interest. After those miners went missing, he scooped them up and locked them down."

"He's not working them?"

"Not as far as I can tell."

"Hasn't anyone else suspected Torquelan of being involved with those miners?" Clint asked.

"Of course. That's when he holed up in them three buildings and stopped talking to anyone apart from his own men and a few of his business associates."

"Which associates?"

"Suppliers and such," Wheeler replied.

Clint swirled what was left of his beer around in his glass. "What do they supply him with?"

"Don't know just yet."

"Where do you intend on going from here?"

"I've got a few ideas, but I've only just started getting my hands dirty on this whole affair. It didn't take much digging for me to find myself in over my head."

"Yeah," Clint sighed. "I know just what you mean."

TWENTY-EIGHT

The sun crested the horizon, bathing Las Primas in its glow. When she awoke, Gigi found herself alone. She emerged from her wagon, looked around, and quickly spotted a familiar pair of boots sticking out from a bedroll that had been spread on the ground beneath a nearby tree. She went over and tugged on one of the boots until the man connected to the feet within them began to stir.

"Do I want to know why you're sleeping out here instead of with me?" she asked.

"Couldn't be certain," Clint said as he sat up and stretched, "but I may have been followed."

"That again? Take it from someone who's been pursued by plenty of men. There comes a time when you've just got to move on with your life and take your chances. If anyone found us here, they'd likely find us anywhere else we tried to hide."

Clint kicked off the blanket and climbed to his feet. "Not hiding," he said. "Laying low. There's a difference."

"Whichever you want to call it, neither one of us is sleeping in a comfortable bed."

"You got me there. If I don't get something in my stomach, I won't be much use to anyone. Some strong coffee wouldn't hurt either."

"I know just the place."

She led Clint to a small hotel that served meals in a dining room with only four tables. Since there were just enough guests to fill half of those tables, they were seated and served in no time at all. There wasn't a menu for them to pick from, but they were brought portions of bacon, browned potatoes, toast, and a mess of scrambled eggs. To wash it down, they were given coffee that Clint could smell even before they'd stepped into the hotel.

"Perfect," he sighed after sipping from the steaming cup he'd been given.

"I knew you'd like it here."

"Advice from the spirits?"

"No," she said. "You're a man. You're happy with food so long as it's piled high and within reach. The coffee is also strong enough to peel paint from a barn door."

"That's always welcome after a hard night's sleep." Clint took a drink of the potent brew, which hit him like a slap in the face.

"Where did you go last night?" Gigi asked.

"To check and see if your house was still standing."

"And was it?"

"Yes," Clint replied. "But just barely."

Her eyes widened into saucers and then narrowed down into slits. "That's not funny."

"It's good to know I can pull one over on a woman who can see the future. I must be talented."

"All right. You made your point."

"Speaking of the future, I want you to tell me exactly what you said to those men who came to you right before these problems with Torquelan started."

Gigi shrugged while poking at her breakfast with a fork. "I already told you that."

"Tell me again. And be exact. Before I do anything else, I want to have overturned every rock to make sure I've found anything and everything that can possibly help me."

"Help you do what exactly?" When Clint didn't answer right away, she gripped her fork a little tighter and said, "You'll have to be exact with me first and then I'll be exact with you."

"I think you're a little too accustomed to working with paying customers."

Gigi let out the breath that had tensed her entire body, then she looked down at her plate.

Even if she was putting on a bit of a performance to get her way, Clint still felt bad for snapping at her. "I can't give you too many details because I simply don't know them yet. All I do know for certain is that I've stumbled into a tangled damned mess in this town and Torquelan is at the center of it. You're wrapped up in it as well, and since you're more likely to talk to me without lying to my face, I'm trying to get as much from you as I can."

"Apology accepted," she said with a little smile.

Clint didn't recall apologizing, but before he knew it, he nodded and told her, "I am sorry, Gigi."

She was good.

Whatever satisfaction she took from the way she'd steered his words in the proper direction didn't last very long. Using her fork to move her food around, she asked, "How big of a mess is it?"

"Pretty big. At first, it just seemed like the men following me were after you or possibly me for some past incident that I forgot about."

"You've made enough transgressions to forget about one that someone might want to kill you for?"

"You'd be surprised," Clint said. "Anyway, now it looks like Torquelan is involved in some kind of scheme with a bunch of different mining claims and he's started surrounding himself with armed men."

"Torquelan's not the only rich man to have done something like that."

"True," Clint admitted, "but none of them thought twice about firing on me and the sheriff when we went to pay them a visit. Granted, the sheriff made something of a bold entrance, but even after announcing himself, those gunhands didn't let up. They meant to kill us, and my gut tells me that would have been the case even if we'd knocked on the door and asked politely to be let inside."

Gigi didn't seem overly frightened by what she heard. Clint's read on her was that she wasn't looking forward to any sort of a fight but wasn't about to run from one either.

"Did anyone mention some miners that had gone missing recently?" she asked.

"Yes. What do you know about them?"

"Nothing," she sighed. "But there were some people who came around to visit me so they could ask about where those miners might be found."

"What did you tell them?" Clint asked, even though he was dreading the answer he might hear.

"I couldn't tell them anything because I didn't know anything. I just . . ." Gigi looked around at the few others having their breakfasts at other tables and then lowered her voice so she couldn't be heard by anyone other than Clint. "I just told them the missing men weren't in any pain and would be found soon. I didn't say if they would be alive or dead. I just . . . didn't know what else to tell them. It's not the first time I've had to lie to someone grieving over a loved one and it's never easy. It's my least favorite thing I have to do in my line of work." Averting her eyes from him, she added, "Now go ahead and tell me how I don't have to lie at all. Especially to people in so much pain."

To her surprise, Clint reached across the table and put his hand upon hers. "It can't be easy," he said, "but what you're providing is a service to those people. You're giving them something. Hope."

"And what if their loved ones are dead? What kind of hope is that?"

"It's the kind that will provide them some measure of comfort. And who's to say if you're not correct in telling them they'll be reunited with them someday?"

"You don't think that notion is a bit . . . quaint?"

"Doesn't matter," Clint said. "It's been working for preachers for a long time, so it must have some kind of foundation."

Gigi smiled at him and went from picking at her food to eating it again. "I think I do remember a few other exact words I told those men."

"Good. Let's hear them."

Closing her eyes, Gigi sat up straight as if the table between her and Clint were the one inside her tent. "I told them that their dealings with the man they were doing business with would end up with . . . fire."

"Fire?"

Slowly, she opened her eyes again. Looking more surprised than Clint, she said, "Yes. Fire."

"Why did you mention fire?"

"Because that's what I saw. Truly. I remember it now. When those men asked me about their business dealings, I saw fire."

"Which men?" Clint asked.

"All of them. All the ones who came to me that I later found were connected to Torquelan. I saw fire, Clint, and it wasn't any sort of act."

"I believe you."

"Really?" she asked as her expression brightened. "You're a believer?"

"Don't get carried away. I believe you right now. That doesn't mean I buy into the whole fortune-telling thing."

Gigi shrugged. "I'll take what I can get. I also told them that the gold in their mines wouldn't end up in anyone's hands. Not theirs and not the man they were dealing with who I now know to be Torquelan."

"Was that a real vision also?"

"Yes," Gigi replied without hesitation. "But I'm not certain what it means. The real visions are like that. Never as clear as the ones I make up." Wincing, she quickly added. "Embellish. Not as clear as the ones I embellish. There's a difference."

"Whatever you say." Clint chuckled. He still couldn't shake the notion that she wasn't lying to him about those genuine visions. What mattered more than him believing her, however, was the fact that Torquelan or someone working for him seemed to believe that she'd seen those things.

And since her visions had obviously stricken a nerve, there must be something to them.

"Where do you go from here?" she asked.

"Sometimes when you're trying to untie a knot, it's easier to just cut straight through the thing instead of trying to figure out how it got so tangled up in the first place. Soon as I finish my breakfast," he told her, "I start cutting."

TWENTY-NINE

It did Clint a world of good to stop trying to untie the knot that was Torquelan's entire business structure. Whatever the man had set up for himself, simple or complicated, wasn't something Clint was likely to uncover in a short amount of time. So he focused instead on what he could see with his own eyes or what he'd already found out during his short stay in Las Primas.

The first thing he did was look into the search for those missing miners. Since that was a mystery that had just come to light in recent days, it wasn't difficult to find folks in town who were willing to talk about it. Clint knew he had to take the stories he collected with a grain of salt, but the basic elements were the same throughout all of them.

Chuck Ainsley, Steven Vester, and Michael Howe were the names of the missing miners. As far as Clint could piece together from the stories he'd heard, all three of the men had gone missing within a week of one another. They were all fairly competent at their craft, and the claims they'd made had panned out well enough for them to earn a living. None of them had struck it rich, however, which made it seem peculiar that Torquelan would go through the trouble of kidnapping or possibly killing them.

Clint wound up at Sweet Caroline's for a beer after spending a good portion of his day wandering about town talking to folks. He'd already spoken to the barkeeps working at most of Las Primas's other saloons, so Clint settled in by asking Barry the same question he'd asked the rest.

"Ainsley, Vester, and Howe?" Barry replied as he set Clint's mug of beer in front of him. "Them three had some mighty bad luck, but it's not like they weren't warned."

"Warned?" Clint asked as he took a long drink. "Warned about them being kidnapped?"

"No, that's not the bad luck I meant. I was talking about the cave-in. I'd bet half a fortune that at least one of them's buried in their own mine."

"Hasn't anyone checked there yet?"

"Sure they did," Barry said with a backhanded wave. "But they didn't look hard enough. Working behind a bar in as many mining towns as I have, a man tends to get a good feel for how these fellas' minds work. Plenty of miners go missing when they strike out on their own to dig on a hunch or they just slip and fall into a pit somewhere."

"What did you mean about a cave-in?" Clint asked to try and get the barkeep's story back on track.

"There was a few cave-ins not long ago. At least one that I know about for certain. It was over at Howe's silver mine. Not too big, but any cave-in can be dangerous."

"Has Howe been seen since the cave-in happened?"

"I think so."

Clint let out a tired sigh.

"But," Barry added, "he could very well have gone back. As for them other two, Dr. Lumier warned them about cave-ins, too."

"Who's Dr. Lumier?"

"Some French fella."

"Besides that," Clint said, trying awfully hard not to reach over the bar and strangle the babbling bartender.

"He came to town some time ago, saying he was from the Federal Office of Mining Regulations."

"Never heard of it."

"That don't mean there ain't one," Barry scolded.

Clint couldn't exactly fault him on that. Moreover, he knew that faulting the barkeep wouldn't do him a lick of good anyway.

"So what did this federal man have to say?" Clint asked.

"Don't rightly know. I wasn't there."

Clint leaned over and spoke as if he was confiding solely in the man standing behind it. "That doesn't mean you didn't hear a thing or two about what happened."

It didn't take long for Barry's face to show a sly grin. "Now that you mention it, I did hear a thing or two. That doctor fella warned about some sort of underground activity that might cause cave-ins. Actually, lots of folks know about that part. But what most of them folks don't know is that Ainsley, Vester, and Howe were the first ones who heard about it. Vester even found a section of his own mine that had collapsed."

"I hadn't heard a thing about that," Clint said. "And I spoke to a man who claimed to have played cards with Vester on a regular basis at a saloon a few streets down."

"Vester only played at that rat trap saloon because he could fleece them drunks for half of what they were worth," Barry grunted. "He came here much more often and he spoke to me about plenty of things. One of them was that this Dr. Lumier was making the rounds talking to some of the local miners about some kind of secret project that'd help in the predictin' of quakes."

"Predicting earthquakes?"

Barry nodded. "The doctor came to me special asking if I could recommend anyone who might be interested in helping test the device he brought along with him. I had a feeling he was fishing for a bribe. He mentioned that the device will benefit all miners once it became used commonly, but could benefit a select few who could use it before anyone else knew about it. Could let them know when to sell a claim, when to buy, when to move on to new ground, that sort of thing."

Clint wasn't a miner by trade, but he could definitely see the possibilities. It didn't take much imagination at all to buy into the notion of a government worker taking advantage of his position by sticking his hand out for a bit of extra profit.

"You said this doctor was using some sort of device?" Clint asked.

Barry tapped his chin. "You know something? I never actually saw it, but I think it was a device. Some sort of machine or measuring instrument, but it sounded convincing to me. It sure would explain the cave-ins at Vester's and Howe's places."

"So you think Ainsley had a cave-in as well?"

Barry shrugged. "Could explain why nobody can find him. Sure, there's already been folks down at his claim, but if it was a smaller cave-in and them folks didn't know exactly where to look . . ."

"Then nobody would find him," Clint said.

"You got it."

"Would you happen to know where those three men's claims are?"

THIRTY

There was still plenty of daylight when Clint reached the mine owned by Michael Howe. It was the closest to town, located just over a mile away tucked in good and tight among some hills. Clint nearly rode past it altogether, even with Barry's directions fresh in his mind. The only sign marking the spot was coated in dirt and halfway overgrown by thorny weeds. After pulling back on his reins, Clint hesitated before climbing down from Eclipse's back.

"You think that's it, boy?" he grumbled. "Sure doesn't look like much."

Eclipse let out a huffing breath and shook his head as if letting Clint know that he agreed with the assessment. After all, they'd found nothing more than a hole in the ground marked by a few planks of wood. Since he'd come this far, though, Clint swung down from his saddle so he could get a closer look.

As he approached the little sign sticking up from the filthy ground, Clint could hear nothing but Eclipse's breaths and those of the wind itself as it rolled across the sunbaked California terrain. Since the sign barely came up to his knees, Clint had to squat down so he could wipe away some of the grit that had collected upon its surface. With the dirt chipped away, he could make out a few words scrawled there in flaking black paint.

PRIVATE PROPERTY—KEEP AWAY

Beneath the warning was a number, possibly one that would match the official claim Michael Howe had filed with the proper authority to make the mine legally his. Clint stepped to one side so his shadow wasn't blocking the mine's entrance. Even with a bit more light shining down on it, the opening didn't look any more appealing.

"How the hell did the owner even find this place?" Clint wondered aloud. "Oh well. I guess this is what I came for."

Clint left Eclipse in a spot where the Darley Arabian could get some measure of shade. From there, he made his way back to the mine entrance and steeled himself for a dirty climb into what could very possibly be a nest of snakes or spiders.

The mine entrance had probably started off as a crack in the rocks. There were still chips and scrapes in those rocks from the tools that had been used to widen the crack into something large enough for a man to get through. Not a large man, but a man all the same. Angled somewhere between fifty and sixty degrees, the entrance made Clint feel unsteady on his feet and expecting to be taken off them at any moment. As he stepped cautiously into the jagged hole, he searched for friendly surfaces with his fingertips as well as anxious toes within his boots.

Once inside the mine, things took a turn for the better. The ground leveled out a bit. The air was cooler. The light was even coming in at a more favorable angle, which allowed him to see a ways into the murky depths. It wasn't the sort of mine that had been worked by any sort of company or team of diggers. There were no tracks on the ground and nowhere near enough space to accommodate a cart. Clint did, however, spot a small pile of tools propped against a portion of rock that folded into something of a natural alcove.

Clint approached the alcove and reached out to trace his hand along the blade of a shovel and the pointed head of a pick. On the ground, tucked in behind the half circle created by the digging tools, was a lantern. Clint picked it up, shook it, and heard there was still some oil left inside. He lit it with a match from his pocket and adjusted the wick until the flame was just high enough for him to move deeper into the mine.

He wasn't looking forward to scraping around inside a series of tunnels, which was fortunate because Clint walked less than twenty paces before hitting a wall. The rocks that had fallen to block the mine shaft were wedged in good and tight. The ground was littered with smaller rocks and layers of chip-filled dust, which made him think some sort of rescue operation had been mounted. At the very least, someone had tried to dig a ways through the barricade.

Something about that didn't set right with Clint. If there had been a rescue, then folks should have been saying Michael Howe was lost in the cave-in rather than simply missing. Turning away from the fallen rock, Clint studied the walls on either side of him.

"What have we here?" he whispered while leaning in for a closer look.

What had caught Clint's attention was the glint of light
from his lantern reflecting against several crooked lines
etched into the stone. He wasn't an expert in such things,
but he was fairly certain he was looking at either silver or
copper ore that was ripe for the picking. But that wasn't
what held his interest. Any man would expect to see ore
inside a mine. He might even expect to see scorch marks
on the walls. Finding scorch marks so close to a pile of
fallen rocks, on the other hand, pointed to something other
than simple blasting. Something had gone wrong.

Blasting accidents weren't unusual. What seemed out
of place in this one was that nobody seemed to have even
mentioned blasting in all the talk Clint had heard of earthquakes and cave-ins.

Suspicion nagged in the back of Clint's mind, but he
didn't know enough to put together anything more than
that. Since there wasn't much else to find in that collapsed
tunnel, he climbed out and headed to the next one.

THIRTY-ONE

Clint arrived at the Vester claim about an hour later. It took him a short while to poke around on uneven terrain and meander along a creek that couldn't flow for more than a couple of yards without a bend. There were signs poking out of the ground occasionally, marking spots claimed in much the same way that Howe had claimed his narrow hole in the ground. These signs, however, were much easier to read.

STAY BACK!! TRESSPASSERS WIL BE SHOT

SMITH AND CORBEN PROPERTY—KEEP OFF!!

LEGAL CLAIM FILED—JUMPERS WONT BE TOLERATED

Clint found a few others, but they all kept to that same theme. Barry had told him he could find the Vester claim on the north side of the trail Clint was riding, so he kept right on moving. Men with long beards and dirty faces poked their heads up like prairie dogs to watch him pass. A few of them hollered for him to stay away, which made them only slightly less helpful than the signs they'd posted.

The rest glared angrily at Clint and then got back to their work once they saw he wasn't going to stop at their claim.

He only had to ride over the next hill before he spotted more signs sprouting like a sporadic crop from parched, stony ground. Just as he was about to give up on sifting through all of those rude and misspelled proclamations, Clint found the one he'd been after. It was about twenty yards from the trail propped against a cave that could have easily been mistaken for a bear's den. When he rode a little closer, Clint could see the jumble of rocks piled high enough to stop up the cave's entrance like a cork.

"Something tells me that's the one I'm looking for," he grumbled.

Clint flicked his reins, rode close enough to read the sign, and then climbed down from his saddle. The cave was marked as belonging to S. VESTER. Apart from the name, there wasn't much else written there. Clint couldn't take a full step into the cave without being stopped by the barricade of rock. He was trying to get a look at the wall surrounding the rock when Eclipse let out a loud, huffing whinny.

Clint continued to prod at some of the rocks to see if they might be loose until he heard the scrape of boots against the ground. Once he had a good idea of where the other person was behind him, he spun around while drawing his Colt in one smooth motion.

The man who approached Clint was one of the prairie dogs who'd watched him ride past earlier. He was covered from head to toe in dirt and mud, carrying only a pick, which he wielded in a vaguely threatening manner. "What the hell you doin' here, mister?" he asked.

"Just having a look at this mine," Clint replied.

"Ain't your mine. That is, unless you can prove your right to it."

"I can't."

The filthy man obviously saw the gun in Clint's hand, but wasn't frightened by it in the slightest. "Then why you here?" he growled.

"Steven Vester is missing," Clint said.

"Any damn fool knows as much."

"I'm here to see what happened to him."

The miner's brow furrowed and he shifted his grip on the pick he carried. "That so?"

"It is."

Clint could feel when he was being scrutinized. It made matters a whole lot easier when he didn't have anything to hide. After coming to a conclusion that was favorable enough for him to lower his pick, the miner said, "You don't look like a lawman."

"That's because I'm not a lawman. I was passing through Las Primas when I seemed to have run afoul of a man who lives there."

"That man got a name?"

"Wilhelm Torquelan."

Clint had barely spoken half of that name when the miner started to nod. "What's that son of a bitch want with you?" the filthy man asked.

"Near as I can tell, he wants to kill me."

The other man smiled, exposing a set of teeth that were even more cracked and dirty than the rocks blocking the cave in front of Clint. "Well then," he said. "I suppose that means you can't be all that bad."

Clint holstered the Colt, even though it hadn't seemed

to make a dent in the other man's behavior anyway. "And who might you be?" he asked.

"Jeb Mattes. I work a claim on the other side of that hill out yonder."

"I'm Clint Adams."

"I'd shake yer hand, Clint, but you'd have to take a bath afterward."

"Understood. What do you know about what happened to Mr. Vester?"

Jeb turned his head so he could spit onto the ground away from the cave. "Damn shame about what happened to him. He was a good man. A mite gullible for this line of work, but a good man."

"Gullible?" Clint asked.

"Everyone in a suit is tryin' to pull the wool over a miner's eyes. Sellin' false claims, stealing legal ones, paying too little for whatever we manage to scrape out of the ground, any number of ways for us to be cheated. A man in this line of work needs to keep a sensible head on his shoulders."

"And Mr. Vester had some trouble in that regard?"

Shrugging, Jeb glanced toward the rocks piled in front of him as if he was being careful not to upset them. "Maybe he was just too optimistic for his own good," he said while reaching out with one hand to pat the closest rock plugging up the cave's entrance.

"I was told he might have been lost in a cave-in."

"Could be."

"You don't believe that," Clint noted.

Jeb gnawed on the inside of one cheek as if he meant to spit that out next.

Measuring every one of the other man's movements, Clint said, "I was also told about a man named Dr. Lumier.

He was supposed to have come around here with some sort of government experiment."

"Yeah," Jeb chuckled. "That character was here all right. And if'n he was a doctor, then I'm a duck. Last I checked, I didn't have no feathers sprouting from my ass."

"Did Vester think any better of him?"

"Hard for anyone to think any worse of someone. Steven didn't buy everything that so-called doctor was sellin', but he was curious enough to let him into his mine. That French doctor fella brought some equipment with him. Looked like a bunch of nonsense and wires to me."

"You saw it?" Clint asked.

"Oh, yeah. We all keep an eye out for anyone comin' along to poke their nose where it don't belong. Most of the men out here lose interest once they know their own claims are safe. I believe in having a bit more watchfulness where neighbors are concerned."

"That's an honorable code to live by."

Scowling, Jeb spat on the ground before saying, "I wasn't watchful enough. That doctor and a few others went down into this cave, and when they came out, Steven was all kinds of flustered. He went on about cave-ins and such, but ain't none of us had any trouble of that sort. At least, not any of us that been takin' proper precautions."

"What does Torquelan have to do with all of this?"

"It was Torquelan's boys that brought that doctor fella around. And it's been Torquelan who's been spreading the word about getting on that doctor's good side so folks can use whatever that contraption is that he brought down into this here mine."

Clint studied the rocks that lay piled directly in front of him. "So you think Vester was buried in the cave-in?"

"If there was a cave-in at all. Y'see, I was workin' my claim the night this mine collapsed. There was a blast. It was muffled. Probably set underground, but I heard it. I saw Vester a few minutes later. He was workin' out here as well and come runnin' when that sound could be heard. There were others pokin' around, too."

"Who were they?" Clint asked. "More of Torquelan's men?"

"I didn't see for certain. At the time, I thought it was any one of these other men who might be workin' their claims. It was gettin' dark at the time, and it was hard to see much more than shapes and such."

"What's your gut tell you?"

Jeb paused, but not to think over his answer. He clearly knew what he wanted to say and only needed to decide if he wanted to say it to Clint. Finally, he told him, "My gut tells me that Steven is either buried in this mine or somewhere else. Either way, he ain't missing. He's dead."

"Just like those other two that nobody's been able to find," Clint said.

"That's right."

"I've got my own problems with Torquelan, but won't trouble you with them," Clint explained. "All I want now is to figure out what Torquelan has in mind. After that, I have a feeling the rest will become clear enough."

"In that case," Jeb said, "you might like to know that French doctor has been spouting off a whole lot about the claim belonging to one of them other missing fellas."

"You mean Michael Howe?"

"Nah," Jeb replied with a shake of his head. "The Howe claim is already collapsed. Ain't nobody was surprised about that, seein' as Howe was lucky to stay alive as long as he did. The man was sloppy. That doctor may have claimed to know there was gonna be a cave-in in that shit hole of a mine, but we all knew something along them lines was comin' anyways. I'm talkin' about Chuck Ainsley."

"What about him?"

"Accordin' to that slick-talkin' doctor, there's supposed to be a cave-in on Chuck's claim the day after tomorrow."

THIRTY-TWO

Clint returned to town in a cloud of dust kicked up by Eclipse's hooves. The Darley Arabian always relished a chance to cut loose and run at a full gallop, and after what he'd heard, Clint was more than happy to oblige. The perimeter of Las Primas was as calm as on the day Clint arrived. On the other side of the coin, the merchant district farther inside the town's limits was just as chaotic.

As soon as he saw the entrance to the wide alleyway that led to Gigi's house, Clint pulled back on Eclipse's reins and swung down from the saddle. Even though he hadn't knocked into anyone along the way, he received enough angry shouts from nearby locals to make it seem as if he'd trampled half of them on his route into town.

Clint snapped his reins like a whip to wrap them around a hitching post in one motion. Knowing the stallion could kick any potential thief into a second-floor window, he left Eclipse to catch his breath without fear.

"You again?" the fish vendor grunted as Clint approached.

"Yeah, it's me," Clint replied. "Has anyone else been around?"

"Plenty! This look like an empty field to you, asshole?"

"What about Madame Giselle's? Anyone been to see her?"

"I would imagine so. With an ass like she's got, there's always plenty of men lining up to have their turn." Before the fish vendor could laugh at his own crude joke, he was fighting to take his next breath.

Clint had lunged at him to grab the fish vendor by the collar in a tight grip. Then, he pulled sharply down to mash the vendor's face into a pile of stinking trout. "That's for insulting the lady," Clint said. "Should I get started on all the times you've insulted me?"

"Didn't mean anything by it," the vendor sputtered.

"I don't like the way you look at me. And since nobody seems to be rushing to your rescue, I'd imagine you're not any politer to anyone else around here."

"Honestly. I didn't mean no offense. Just . . . just keeping an eye out is all."

"Like a watchdog," Clint offered.

The fish vendor rose up to snap at the hook he'd been given almost immediately. "Yeah! That's right. Like a watchdog!"

Clint had the gruff vendor pegged that way since the first time he'd laid eyes on him. If he wanted that watchdog to stop barking at him and obey his command, Clint needed to find a way to bring him over to his side. As with any other dog, stepping up and showing it who was the master was usually the best tactic.

"Since you've got your eyes open," Clint said, "then maybe you've seen something useful."

"I seen everything that comes up and down this alley. You can believe that."

"What about any men who work for Wilhelm Torquelan?"

Before the vendor could answer, Madame Giselle herself emerged from her tent. "Clint!" she said. "What are you doing?"

"Having a talk with your neighbor," Clint replied.

She approached them and put a hand on Clint's chest to try and move him away from the fish cart. Clint wasn't allowing himself to be moved, so she did her best to get between them. "Whatever fight you two are having, I'm sure it can be resolved some other way," she said.

"No fight," Clint said without taking his eyes off the man in front of him. "Not yet. He was going to tell me if Torquelan or any of his men were here recently."

"They weren't," Gigi said. "Patrick or I would have—"

"About an hour ago," the fish vendor said. "That crooked government man . . ."

"Dr. Lumier?" Clint asked.

"That's the one. Him and the fancy-looking gunman who works with Mason from time to time. Darrow is his name."

Clint let go of the vendor and turned to Gigi. "That's it," he said. "We're getting away from here."

She wasn't about to argue.

THIRTY-THREE

After a fast and convoluted walk through town, Clint and Gigi wound up in a rented room on the upper floor of Sweet Caroline's. Theirs was one of only three rooms up there and the only one that was occupied. It was sparsely furnished, relatively clean, and had a window overlooking the street.

"You drug me up and down nearly every alleyway in Las Primas just to wind up here?" Gigi asked.

Clint stood at the narrow window, peeling back the curtain just enough to get a look outside. "Had to make sure we weren't followed," he said.

Settling on the bed, Gigi looked around the room. "I didn't even know there were rooms to rent in here."

"Most saloons have at least a few rooms for customers too drunk to get home."

"Or for a place to take whores."

Since there was nobody outside that seemed overly suspicious, Clint pulled the curtain back so it covered the entire window. "I know I dragged you away from your place pretty quickly and haven't offered much in the way of an explanation, but there's good reason."

"I'm listening."

"I think Torquelan will try to kill you."

Gigi nodded.

"You don't seem surprised," Clint said.

"His gunmen keep lurking around. You keep getting attacked. It only makes sense."

"Do you know why this is happening?"

"Other than what you've already told me? No."

Clint believed her. "Torquelan is running some sort of scheme involving local miners and some government man. Actually, I doubt he's really with the government at all. Anyway, he's been blowing up mines and trying to pass them off as cave-ins."

"So that's why he got so upset when I told those men about their business dealings ending in fire?" she asked.

"I'd say so."

A wide smile made its way onto her face. "That's great!"

"Huh? Why is that great?"

"Because it means that I'm having more visions. *Real* visions. This is so exciting!"

"I'm glad one of us is so happy," Clint grumbled.

"I know the rest isn't so good," she said as she approached him. "But I also know you'll take care of me. Somehow I knew that from the first moment I saw you." Gigi placed her hands on his back and slowly rubbed his shoulders. "I just knew to trust you."

"Then perhaps you'll listen to me when I tell you to stay here until I settle this matter with Torquelan."

"Is that an order?"

Clint faced her and put his hands on her hips. "Yeah. I'm afraid it is. Less chance of you getting hurt that way."

Nodding once, she said, "Then that's what I'll do."

"That was easy."

"Why do you sound so surprised?"

"Because you haven't struck me as the sort of woman who does anything the easy way," Clint said.

"Maybe I just like things to be hard." Gigi reached between Clint's legs, felt his erection start to grow, and smiled up at him. "Yes. I do like them hard."

"When I say I wanted you to stay here, that meant you'd stay after I left."

"I realize that," she whispered while unbuckling his belt. "And since I might not see you again after this business is through, I thought I'd give you a proper good-bye." Gigi lowered herself to her knees, taking Clint's pants down along the way. His rigid cock was directly in front of her red lips as she looked up to him and said, "That is, if you have time for me?"

"Oh, I think I can spare a moment or two."

THIRTY-FOUR

Gigi's lips curled into a sly grin as she opened her mouth and took him inside. Clint only felt the warmth of her breath until he was mostly in her mouth. Then, she closed her lips around him and pressed her tongue against his hard shaft. Clint pulled in a deep breath while placing his hands on the back of her head. That way, he could guide her as she started to bob her head back and forth.

Her rhythm was slow at first, sliding up and down along his cock. As she sucked him faster, she flicked her tongue on him. Gigi reached around to grasp Clint's hips and surprised him by taking him all the way down to the back of her throat. Once there, she stayed put while letting out a deep moan that sent chills up Clint's spine.

When she pulled back, Gigi looked up at him and allowed him to slip from her mouth. She then pressed her lips together and ran them along his length so he could feel their smooth, wet surface from tip to base. Gigi opened her mouth and sucked him again. This time when she eased up, Clint started pumping. She responded to that by holding her head still and taking every inch that he fed to her.

Before long, Clint wanted more. He took a step back, helped her stand up, and began peeling off her clothes. Gigi swiftly undressed him at the same time, until they both stood there naked, each probing the other's body with eager hands. Clint reached between her legs and found her pussy to be warm and slick with moisture. As soon as his fingers touched her there, she let out a deep-throated moan.

Clint took her in his arms and backed her against a wall. The instant her shoulders hit the wooden slats, Gigi rubbed one leg against him and ground herself against his stiff cock. She was practically climbing up his body by the time Clint reached down to cup her buttocks in both hands and lift her up. As soon as both of Gigi's feet left the floor, she wrapped her legs around him and held on tight.

Gigi kissed his neck and chewed on Clint's earlobe as he reached down to guide his rigid penis to where they both wanted it to be. When he felt her pussy lips against the tip of his cock, he thrust forward to bury himself deep inside her.

"Yes, Clint," she moaned while clawing his back. "Give it to me. Give it all to me."

Clint pounded into her again and again, handing himself over to every animal instinct that flowed through his body. His hands tightened around her ass, cupping her plump buttocks to hold her steady as he drove into her again. Gigi arched her back as far as she could, rubbing her erect nipples against Clint's chest.

Soon, Clint moved away from the wall to hold her in place. She used her entire body to bounce on his rigid cock, wrapping her legs around him with all her strength. Before Clint's knees buckled, he sat down on the bed and took her right along with him. Gigi wasted no time at all before placing her hands upon his chest and shoving him down to lie on his back.

She smiled once again, leaning her head back while slowly grinding on his cock. Clint ran his hands along her thighs, feeling the muscles work beneath her skin as she built up to a more urgent pace. Every time she took him inside her, Gigi let out a short grunt. Those sounds built into a quick staccato as she rode him harder and faster.

For a while, Clint lay back and savored the feel of her weight on top of him, the warmth of her body pressed against his, and the dampness between her thighs, which only grew wetter the more she worked. Then, he let his eyes wander along the front of her body. Gigi's firm tits bounced in time to her rhythm and her nipples had become fully erect. Little beads of sweat ran between them, and as she let out a groaning breath, she ran the tip of her tongue against her lips.

"You like that?" she asked.

Clint wasn't certain what, exactly, she was referring to but it didn't really matter. "Yes, I like it," he growled. "Don't stop."

Grinning with the knowledge that she was making him feel just as good as she felt, Gigi leaned her weight forward to rest it upon her arms. Her hands mashed against his chest, allowing her to pump her hips faster. While her upper body remained mostly still, her lower body moved like a piston as she impaled herself on him again and again.

Clint could feel every movement flood through his

body. Heat from her glistening flesh rolled over him and the air was filled with her scent. He grabbed her hips tighter and stared straight into her eyes as he started to drive up into her.

Digging her nails into Clint's chest, Gigi hung on to him as he pounded between her thighs. Before long, her entire body shuddered with a climax, which lasted until Clint's pleasure reached its peak. With one last thrust, he exploded inside her. Now that both of them were spent, Gigi lay on top of him like a wilted flower, too tired to move.

"Does making a fortune-teller feel that good grant me special favors from the spirits?" Clint asked.

"If it does," she gasped, "you're going to be one lucky man for a very long time."

THIRTY-FIVE

It was just past dawn the following day and Wilhelm Torquelan had been up for hours. He didn't normally get up so early, but today was a day for conducting business, which meant it would require some extra attention. There would be visitors coming, frightened locals, curious officials, and any number of unforeseen turns to navigate. At the end of it, he would be richer than he was right now. That's all that mattered to him.

He smiled to himself in the little round shaving mirror hanging above the wash basin in his bedroom. The straight razor in his hand scraped away another layer of lather and whiskers, leaving only a narrow strip of his chin left to do when someone walked in looking even better than he did.

"What is it, Darrow?" Torquelan asked.

"You might want to go down to the Ainsley spread."

"That's quite all right. I'm sure you men can handle the job. It's best I look fresh to receive any—"

"No," Darrow interrupted. "There's been a problem."

Torquelan's hand froze with the razor poised above his Adam's apple. "What kind of a problem? Have the packages been delivered?"

"They're being held back, sir. That's the problem."

"Held back? How?"

"It's Adams," Darrow replied crisply.

Resuming the last few swipes of his shave, Torquelan said, "I'm sure you men can handle him. If all else fails, just blow him to hell when you destroy the mine."

"That's just it, sir. The package hasn't been delivered yet."

This time when Torquelan froze, he stopped just short of digging the blade into his own flesh. "It was supposed to have been delivered hours ago."

"I know. Adams was there before us. For all we know, he was sleeping there just waiting for us to—"

"I don't give a damn if he decided to live in one of those fucking mines! There's no reason . . . no reason in hell . . . why you men couldn't have moved him! I sent at least ten of you out there in case there was trouble."

"We lost some when Adams and the sheriff came along," Darrow reminded him.

"But that still leaves enough men to handle one. Or is it more than one?" Torquelan let out a labored sigh before asking, "Did your men fail to clear away the goddamn miners as well?"

"There weren't any miners around. It's just Adams."

"What about the sheriff? He's become a pain in the ass as well."

"I didn't see him, sir. When we arrived, Adams was there. He told us to turn back and leave the package where it was. When we tried to clear him out, he brought down two of us. When we tried to bring the delivery any closer to the mines, he threatened to destroy it."

"Son of a bitch!" Torquelan howled as he threw his razor with enough force to break it on impact when it hit the wall. "What the hell does this cocksucker want?"

"I have an idea, sir, but he wasn't saying for certain. The only way to find out is for you to go there and ask him yourself."

"Are you trying to tell me what to do?" Torquelan asked in a low snarl.

"No, sir," Darrow replied in the same even tone he used when saying anything else. "I'm just relaying a message. Adams specifically said he wanted you to go out there and have a word with him or he would burn down your entire operation."

"He did, did he? Well, I don't take orders from anyone, especially some stranger who's barely been here long enough to know one end of town from the other. I pay you and the rest of the men to handle problems like him so you all get your asses back to that mine and handle it!"

"Yes, sir. Where are you going?"

"I'm going to handle my end of the business. We all do our jobs no matter what. That's how jobs get done. Understand?"

Darrow nodded, turned on his heel, and left.

THIRTY-SIX

Clint stood at the top of a small rise overlooking Chuck Ainsley's claim. Before arriving, he'd had a word with Jeb, who agreed to convince any other miners who might be in the area to find somewhere else to be for a spell. The wagon driven by Mason had arrived a bit earlier than Clint was expecting, but that only meant he had less time to wait before meeting it.

One man lay dead in the dirt halfway between Clint and the wagon. He'd been the one sent to force Clint to leave or bury him in the mine along with the packages meant for delivery on the back of the wagon. That man had had a fairly fast gun hand, but it wasn't fast enough. After that man dropped from one shot from Clint's Colt, Darrow had been willing to hear Clint out.

"Looks like Darrow's on his way back," Clint announced.

Apart from Mason, who sat in the wagon's driver's seat, there were three gunmen remaining. They'd fanned out to gain the best position they could and Clint had let them.

"He's riding alone," Clint added. "Looks like Torquelan wasn't interested in hearing me out. That also means he wasn't interested in stopping any more blood from getting spilled."

Not one of the men in that standoff was surprised by that.

"Shows you the sort of man you're working for," Clint said. "He'd rather send you to be shot or killed than lift a finger to look out for you."

Darrow rode closer. He'd close to within a hundred yards in less than a minute.

"Then again," Clint continued, "I suppose none of you are the sort who would look out for anyone. You've killed at least three miners, blown up two claims, and for what? To prove a point? To let Torquelan put a few more dollars into his pockets?"

"Step away from there and let us pass," Mason said. "I won't ask again."

Clint nodded. "You're right. This is well past the talking stage. You want to do what you came to do? You'll have to go through me. Otherwise, turn back and scurry on home."

Clint's choice of words had been well crafted. His intention was to quit waiting for Darrow to arrive and get the others to jump if they were going to jump.

He succeeded.

The first one to move was Mason. He snapped his reins and got the wagon's team moving while barking at the horses in a loud, choppy voice. All of that was more than enough to signal the other three gunmen to make their move.

Clint watched this unfold while waiting for the last possible moment in which to act. He wanted to give the men a chance to back away from the fight, but he wasn't about to stand still and allow any of them to get a lucky shot. Fortunately, any dilemmas were cast aside because all of the men went for their guns.

Two of the three gunmen cleared leather at roughly the same time. Clint pulled his Colt from its holster and sent a round burning through the first one's chest. Before that one fell over, Clint was taking aim at the next.

The second of the two quicker draws pulled his trigger when he should have squeezed. His hasty mistake caused his first shot to be pulled down and to the right, where it dug a hole into the ground a few yards behind Clint's position.

Clint fired at the next closest target, which happened to be the man who was last to draw his pistol. That shooter had the presence of mind to drop into a one-kneed firing stance, which prolonged his life for another couple of seconds. Clint's round hissed through the air a few inches away from his left ear as the gunman sent a round back at him.

Hot lead nipped at Clint's elbow like an animal's claw that had snagged his shirt on its way past him. The grazing shot barely registered in his head, but it did manage to send his next shot wide. Clint rolled with the slight impact by shifting into a sideways stance. From there, he straightened his arm and fired his last two rounds in quick succession.

The first bullet drilled through one gunman's eye.

The second blasted apart a large piece of the other gunman's neck.

Both men fell straight to their backs, where they took their first steps into the great beyond.

The wagon was still coming toward the mine and Darrow was swiftly approaching the wagon. Clint calmly strode over to the gunmen he'd just killed, picked up the pistols they'd dropped, and opened fire. Thunder roared from both fists as the pistols bucked against his palms. Accuracy wasn't much of a concern since his target was damn hard to miss.

Mason kept hold of his reins and hunched down low once he realized that Clint's bullets were coming his way. The board behind him was torn apart by incoming lead. Moments later, the first few rounds hit their true mark.

Stacked in the back of the wagon were three crates filled with dynamite. Clint couldn't know for certain whether he'd hit one of them square or if his gunfire had sparked a blaze somewhere along the line, but it didn't really matter. One of the crates exploded, which ignited the rest of the cargo. Within seconds, the entire wagon was engulfed in a fireball and the resulting blast filled Clint's ears with a powerful ringing.

Darrow had attempted to veer away from the wagon and had even managed to create a bit of distance between it and him before the crates had gone up. There was no way, however, for him or any horse to outrun the jagged chunks of wood and iron shrapnel that were sent flying in all directions. Even Clint received a good amount of bloody gashes from flying debris. Darrow, on the other hand, had his pretty face separated from his head. He surely had other parts removed in an ugly manner, which didn't matter in the slightest.

Dead was dead.

Clint stood up, dusted himself off, and walked down the other side of the rise, where Eclipse was safely tethered.

THIRTY-SEVEN

Torquelan arrived at a small hotel on the outskirts of town in a rush. He stormed inside, started to go upstairs, and then spotted what he was after in a different location. He passed the front desk and stomped over to a thin, bespectacled man sitting at one of the tables where complimentary breakfast was served to guests.

"Come on," Torquelan said. "We've got work to do."

"You're not going anywhere," Sheriff Wheeler announced.

The man at the table didn't know what to do as Torquelan spun around to face the lawman, who stood behind him near the front desk. When the hotel clerk started to speak, Wheeler motioned for him to stand back.

"You're Dr. Lumier, right?" Wheeler asked.

The bespectacled man at the table nodded. "I am."

"Let's see your credentials."

"Excuse me?"

"If you're a doctor, you must have credentials. Let's see them."

"I am a representative of the Federal Office of Mining Regulations," Lumier announced.

"Then you should have even more credentials."

Facing the lawman, Torquelan said, "You'd better have just cause for this kind of treatment."

"Just cause?" Wheeler growled. "How about fraud, destruction of property, claim jumping, and murder?"

Lumier slowly rose to his feet. "I think I'll just go back to my room now."

Slapping his hand on the gun at his hip, Wheeler said, "Stay put! You're in this just as deep as Torquelan."

"I . . . I can tell you what Mr. Torquelan wanted to do. I can tell you where those miners are buried. I can—"

"Shut your goddamn mouth!" Torquelan roared.

Wheeler grinned. "I already have a real good idea of what Mr. Torquelan wanted to do."

"You don't know shit," Torquelan said.

"You make your money collecting gold claims and rights to as many mines as you can," Wheeler said. "Like any greedy piece of shit, you're not satisfied with the money you've got, so you plan to make more. You do that by bringing in some idiot claiming to have a federally funded machine or study or whatever the hell it is so you can put the scare into the miners around here. You start spreading fear about cave-ins by causing a few cave-ins of your own. That's fraud.

"Even if miners don't believe you, it doesn't matter," Wheeler continued. "Because you still blew up those mines, which makes your intentions clear to anyone who won't sell you their claims or do whatever else you want. That's theft and putting good honest folks in fear for their lives."

"You can't prove any of this," Torquelan said.

Clint had been standing in the doorway of the hotel for

a few seconds and announced himself by saying, "I've got witnesses who saw your men trying to blow up the Ainsley mine while also trying to kill me in the process. Trying," he added, "and failing."

"You men still don't know a damned thing," Torquelan said.

"I'll be your witness as well," Lumier said. "Just, please, get me away from him and see to it that I don't rot in a jail cell."

Torquelan turned toward the bespectacled man. "You spineless, yellow-bellied worm."

"He doesn't want to rot in a cage," Wheeler said. "Or swing from a rope. Can't say as I blame him. You actually had most of your angles figured, I'll give you that much, Wilhelm. You could either con miners out of their claims by selling them cheap before the cave-ins happened, get them to pay for information or expert help from your federal man over there, or just threaten them outright to leave before they were killed next."

"Also," Clint added, "his own business position grew stronger every time one of the mines owned by other men was wiped out."

Wheeler nodded. "I hadn't thought of that. You're coming with me now. Both of you."

"I . . . I'm coming, too?" Lumier whined. "To . . . to . . ."

"So long as you tell everything you know to a judge, I'll see to it you get some measure of leniency."

"That's all I ask," Lumier said with a relieved sigh.

Torquelan's eyes smoldered with rage, but he allowed Wheeler to claim the gun he carried. "You men will regret this," he said through clenched teeth. "Odds are, you won't live to see tomorrow."

Clint, Wheeler, and even Lumier beat those odds.

Torquelan had no friends or hired guns left to help make his threats come to pass. He stood trial, and he alone answered for all of the crimes he'd committed.

Lumier didn't stop talking until the trial was through. and he'd wrangled himself a deal that ended with a short term in a Colorado prison.

Clint made his way back to Las Primas on several occasions to have his palm read . . . among other things.

Watch for

DEATH IN THE FAMILY

399th novel in the exciting GUNSMITH series
from Jove

Coming in March!

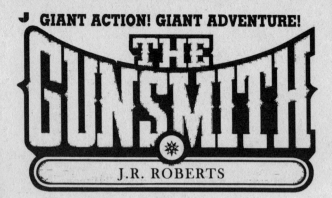

GIANT ACTION! GIANT ADVENTURE!

THE GUNSMITH

J.R. ROBERTS